ONCE UPON A TIME

SOUTH WEST TALES

Edited by Lisa Adlam

First published in Great Britain in 2016 by:

Young**Writers**

Remus House
Coltsfoot Drive
Peterborough
PE2 9BF
Telephone: 01733 890066
Website: www.youngwriters.co.uk

Printed and bound in the UK by BookPrintingUK
Website: www.bookprintinguk.com

FOREWORD

Welcome, Reader!

For Young Writers' latest competition, **Once Upon A Time**, we gave school children nationwide the tricky challenge of writing a story with a beginning, middle and an end in just 100 words, and they rose to the challenge magnificently!

We chose stories for publication based on style, expression, imagination and technical skill. The result is this entertaining collection full of diverse and imaginative mini sagas, which is also a delightful keepsake to look back on in years to come.

Here at Young Writers our aim is to encourage creativity in children and to inspire a love of the written word, so it's great to get such an amazing response, with some absolutely fantastic stories. This made it a tough challenge to pick the winners, so well done to Mitchell White who has been chosen as the best author in this anthology. You can see the winning story on the front cover.

I'd like to congratulate all the young authors in Once Upon A Time - South West Tales - I hope this inspires them to continue with their creative writing. And who knows, maybe we'll be seeing their names on the best seller lists in the future...

Jenni Bannister

Editorial Manager

CONTENTS

THE
MINI SAGAS

The Monster Of The Reeds

Boom! The so-called monster of the reeds roared. I landed in the reeds, my long knobbly legs walking a steady pace. *Boom!* I froze as birds of every kind flew up and scattered into the sky. *Boom!* This was no place for a heron like me. I joined the gaggling gang of birds fleeing. *Boom!* It roared again. This time it emerged from the reeds. This brown, black-spotted creature crept out of its newly claimed territory and *boom!* That's the sound this creature made, way smaller than the heron, way bigger than a thrush. *Boom!* It was a bittern.

Caitlin Keep (11)
Cam Woodfield Junior School, Dursley

AmyLee And The Destroying Marienette

Underneath the deep, eerie sea was an enchanted castle. It was decorated with starfish and glowing coral. Inside lived a mermaid, her name was AmyLee. She lived with her best friend, Rosie.
One day, AmyLee and Rosie went outside of the castle so they could go on an adventure.
A few minutes later, they found a cave. In this cave was a black and grey octopus, her name was Marienette.
'Hello, children,' shouted Marienette, 'would you like to battle me?'
AmyLee said, 'No!' A fireball shot. AmyLee and Rosie grabbed their magic wands and hit her with magic, twice.

Harley Atkinson (11)
Cam Woodfield Junior School, Dursley

Jack's Sea Tragedy

Jack sank deep into the sea. He saw the capsized boat above him. Supplies were drifting through the water. Jack tried to swim up to the vessel. It was Jack's 21st birthday. It was getting desperate now. He had one push to break the surface. He put a tired hand on the rim of the boat. Panting, he felt a tug on his leg. He squealed. He peered down. It was Callum, the unlucky sailor. A tired hand dragged him up to safety. The two of them were on the bottom of the boat watching the bobbing, wooden supply crates.

Aidan Hughes (10)
Cam Woodfield Junior School, Dursley

Every Instrument

Nerves are building. The oboe plays a ringing sound. We are all tuned. Flutes, clarinets, bassoons are all ready. The cor Anglais is warming up. Buzzing quietly, the trumpet is practising. The double bass and violins plucking and bowing as the fife makes a piercing scream in the piccolo's ear. Tubas, trombones, baritones and French horns are all jamming to the hardest piece we have ever played. Now I am raised. Everything goes quiet. In just three bars' time, the whole orchestra will rely on me. I feel a bit sick but I can do it. Right then, here goes!

Isabel Allard (10)
Cam Woodfield Junior School, Dursley

Robo-Drome

One day in the Robo-Drome, Robocrash and Smasherbot were ramming each other, denting each other with their wrecking balls and mallets. Suddenly, Robocrash's wrecking ball went right through Smasherbot's bodywork! The match was won. But Smasherbot couldn't be repaired and was sent to the scrapyard, a place dreaded by all robots. When Buzzsaw and his twin, Ripsaw, found out, they upgraded their weapons and Robocrash did the same because they were going to save Smasherbot. Off they drove into the maze of scrap.

A few hours later, they found Smasherbot. He was lying on his side, dead and defeated.

William Dowler (10)
Cam Woodfield Junior School, Dursley

Untitled

Once there was a teenager called Jeff. There was JimBob, also Rhyle, they were awesome people. They helped people and saved them. Rhyle was a dog, he was trained by Jeff every day. Jeff, Rhyle and JimBob lived in the jungle near houses where people lived and they liked them. Wolves attacked the people and the boys saved them, the people called them heroes. The boys just noticed that there was a person that was controlling the wolves and he had an army. They had a big battle. It was really tough to win it. Luckily they won it.

Brandon Allen (10)
Cam Woodfield Junior School, Dursley

The End

It is 1918 in the northern French trenches where the battle is now decelerating quickly. *Boom! Boom! Boom!* is the loud, deafening sound of the German shells. *Bang! Bang!* is the not so deafening sound of the British guns. Suddenly, a head pops up out of the German trench. 'Halt!' It's the German commander. He hoists himself up from the muddy floor. Jim raises his gun and shoots the feisty commander. 'Argh!' echoes through the sky. The soldiers proceed towards the commander.
'We are finished in this war, you win!' That is the end.

Ben Alexander Lane (10)
Cam Woodfield Junior School, Dursley

The Deserted Patch Of Earth

On a deserted area of the Earth, an ancient man wandered to a pile of bones. The man fell to dried ground, he quickly buried an object. As time ran out, he fell to dust. In the wilderness, a young adult named Alfie sat in his tree house miserably. He felt the need for an adventure. Alfie observed a map and saw a deserted area off the coast of North America, Salt Plains was its name. Before he knew it, he was on his way to the salt plains. When he arrived, he tripped over and spotted a blue cloth...

Sam Bargna (11)
Cam Woodfield Junior School, Dursley

Vampire Virus

The murky Earth was full of man-eating vampires. The human population decreased and the vampire population increased. What caused this? Friday, 16th October 2017 the live broadcast in Germany advised all the countries on Earth the virus started in Africa. Three men from France, who were well skilled in the arts of fighting, were sent to deal with the vampires. I've seen people evolve into deadly vampires. The way you turn into a vampire is when you get bitten by one of them. I've seen many people turn right before my eyes. I'm hiding in an old dark bank...

James Ryan Cordrey (11)
Cam Woodfield Junior School, Dursley

The Chicken Who Ate Chicken

One hot day, a chicken said to himself, 'I fancy something different today.' So he went to the bus stop and he wanted the bus to come. He got on the bus.
Time passed and he finally arrived at McDonald's. He went in and said, 'Please can I have three boxes of chicken nuggets?'
The cashier said, 'OK, I will get them.'
Time passed and he got his food. He took them and ate them. He ate one box then the rest. 'These are good, what are they made of?'
The cashier said, 'This is made of chicken...!'

Luke Gough (11)
Cam Woodfield Junior School, Dursley

The Haunted Church

I am teleported into this building which looks like a church! I don't know what to do, I'm stuck in here! All I can hear is *woooo*. It's getting on my nerves. I look behind me, 'Argh!' There is a ghost so I run as fast as I can. I find a cupboard. I get in it hoping he doesn't find me. I get out. I'm safe now or am I? I go to the graveyard, it is all the dead soldiers that fought in WW2. What the? They come back to life. Am I going to escape them?

Billy Zheng (10)
Cam Woodfield Junior School, Dursley

The Haunted House

The clock struck 12. It was a stormy night when Fred went to visit. He knocked on the door, no one answered. He walked in cautiously. It looked very suspicious as if someone had broken in. He walked into the bedroom where his friend slept, it was just pitch-black. Fred heard a noise downstairs. He ran to see what was there, he looked around - nothing. He shouted his friend's name, nothing. A dark shadow formed on the wall moving towards the doorway. His friend's clothes dangled from the door frame, his name on the wall in blood. Adam!

Mitchell White (10)
Cam Woodfield Junior School, Dursley

The Curious Painting

There was a painting which was moved into a dark, secluded, isolated building about a week ago. I couldn't help myself. I had to go in and have a look. There it was, staring down at me. Suddenly, the eyes of the old man started to pop out, his hands started to try and grab me. Luckily I escaped but the next day on the news, a child who went into the same building as I did, went missing. What will this devil plan to do next? What will this evil do next? What will the future do next?

Bradley Nash (11)
Cam Woodfield Junior School, Dursley

'I Can See You...'

I look around me. It's strangely cold in my room, even though I stoked the blazing fire just a minute ago. The lace curtains at the windows thrash in the wind. Flustered, I run to close the shutters. An antique vase above the mantel falls and smashes on the coal scuttle. The door of the wardrobe slams shut with a thud. Armed with an umbrella from the stand and grasping the kettle tightly, I open the door not daring to breathe... nothing! Suddenly, I am tugged violently inside and hear a faint voice whisper menacingly, 'I can see you...'

Zoë Clutterbuck (10)
Cam Woodfield Junior School, Dursley

Get Me Out Of This Nightmare!

I was reading a story and when I got to page seven, there was a knock at the door. I went to answer the door. There was no one there. So I went back to my room to find blood on the wall. I thought to myself, *how did that get there?* So I went to my mum and dad's room. When I got there, I found a scary monster. I quickly ran out the house. I did not look back. I just kept running. I got to the graveyard. I saw something moving, it was the monster! 'Argh! Help...'

Hanna Dolder (9)
Cam Woodfield Junior School, Dursley

Haunted

The creaky old door slowly opened. I sat up straight as if I had been stung. A shadow leapt up on the cream wall, then disappeared. I got out of bed cautiously and went to the door. My hand was shaking as I reached for the brass doorknob. There I was, standing in front of my door not knowing what was behind the door and not knowing what was in the ramshackle house. Then, without any warning, my arm jerked back. I closed my eyes, too frightened to look. I felt silly but my fright was overpowering my braveness.

Noah Hunter
Cam Woodfield Junior School, Dursley

The Decision

I was stuck. I didn't know where to go. I didn't know what was going on. I could only see little fluffy devils slapping and haunting me. My mind was rushing. People were looking at me like I was a freak, falling on the floor screaming. I tried hiding but it wasn't good enough, they found me every time. Eventually, I came to the forest. Somehow the devils couldn't get into the forest, there was some sort of shield. I thought I was safe. I wasn't. It was the wrong decision. I screamed out loud, 'Help!' Then even louder, *'Help!'*

Phoebe Booth (10)
Cam Woodfield Junior School, Dursley

The Day When People Were No More

As I arrived at my destination, all I could see was the crystal-clear seawater, the scorching sun beaming down on me and the relaxed sunbathers. When I had put my luggage away, I sat on the golden sands as it went through my little toes. Suddenly, everyone had just vanished. As quick as a flash, to wake myself up, I washed my face in the salty sea. After that, I looked up. I couldn't believe my eyes. From being in the sea, I was now in a magical forest! Plants could move! How impossible. Suddenly... 'Help! Help!'

Amy Louise Quemby (11)
Cam Woodfield Junior School, Dursley

The Creature

I ran away, deep into the forest. And to think, I was a scholarship girl. My blue dress flailed behind me as I ran miles, all the way through the forest, until I saw daylight. Then I realised I was being chased. By what? I think it was a bit like a snow leopard, but bigger and scarier. Its red eyes glowed like lamps of fire and its fur was bloody. It was 1913 and nothing like this had happened before, as far as I was aware. I spied a cliff. Jump and I could end the chase. Would I?

Heather Melvill (10)
Cam Woodfield Junior School, Dursley

The Enchanted Woods

Once upon a time there were two poor boys and they went into the abandoned forest to look for food. They stumbled to the other side of the abandoned forest. They fell into a dark abyss. Everything was pitch-black. They got up and started walking and then they started seeing light. They were in the woods again. They looked around. They started to see lots of extinct animals which were very fat. Then they saw this bright light, so they started walking to it. They got closer...

James Hetherington (11)
Cam Woodfield Junior School, Dursley

The Scare Of War

The clash of swords deafened the countryside as the two armies advanced on each other preparing for the upcoming bloodshed. Neither side were ready for the death that was sure to come. No one thought that they would be in this, but they were. Although the sides had quarrelled, they did not wish for war. Argument and disagreement never led to good times in those kingdoms. The winning side was not clear to see but each side tried with all their power. Many weapons caused death on the land and because of this, the winner of the war was war.

Owen Jones (11)
Cam Woodfield Junior School, Dursley

Something Wrong!

On the 1st July at midnight, I suddenly awoke with a start. I felt as if something was wrong, something was missing. I got up and crept into Mum and Dad's bedroom. The bed was empty. I ran downstairs calling for them, no answer. Then I saw a letter nailed to the door. 'Dear Rosie, I have your mum and dad. I am going to get you next'. I ran up to my room and hid under the covers. The door creaked open...

Rosie Cowle (10)
Cam Woodfield Junior School, Dursley

The World Of Elements

I've been here for some time now. I don't know who or what they are. Here they come. They're taking me away from my cage. Where am I being moved to and why? Now I know where I am heading to... the elemental pits of water, fire, soil, with diamond and rock and finally air. Am I going to die? Here I am at the pits, ready to jump and die. Death will be with me. Here I go with the others. Wait, they want me to be a servant. Oops. Accidental death. Goodbye, cruel world.

Alistair Derbyshire (10)
Cam Woodfield Junior School, Dursley

Mushy And Joe Get Lost

Once upon a time, there were three horses called Joe, Mushy and Haggis. Mushy was very naughty so was Joe and they got a smack on the bottom! It was very painful!
One day, Mushy told Joe that Susie was not looking. Mushy said, 'Joe, run away.'
They unbolted the doors and ran like lightning had struck them. They ran and ran until they could go no further and collapsed to the ground. When they got up they saw they were... lost! But not for long. Mushy saw a house and went inside. Mushy and Joe saw beds and slept.

Meghan Goodwin (8)
Cherhill CE Primary School, Calne

Underwater Land

Once upon a time in a magical kingdom, there was a beautiful mermaid called Ariel. There was also a very handsome king called Simon who saved Ariel.
One day, Ariel decided to go to the beach. Just then, she went to the sea. Suddenly, her tail went crazy! She got stuck so she called, 'Help!'
Her tail was stuck underneath a rock and she was unhappy. Her tail was aching. Just then she heard someone saying, 'Don't worry, I'll save you.' Then they got married and had a baby. They called it Olivia Ellen.

Hannah Ellen Pocock (9)
Cherhill CE Primary School, Calne

The Old Wooden Cupboard

One day, Peter was going to school. Suddenly, he found an old wooden cupboard. Silently, Peter went to investigate. Then he got taken to Narnia. Peter was there whilst a battle was going on and he met Prince Caspian. Peter and Caspian went to battle with the Narnians. Only 100 returned.
'When they attack, we will avenge them, so let the battle commence.'
The battle took a while. They celebrated after the battle, knowing they had avenged the other Narnians. Peter went back to the present time and unfortunately, back to school.

James Cuthbert (9)
Cherhill CE Primary School, Calne

Another Earth

Crash!
'Cadet, cadet, cadet!'
'What?' he said, getting up.
'Calm down. Do you know where we are?'
'Maybe.'
'We are on Earth. Everything on this planet has evolved to kill humans. Get a beacon. The Erser escaped. Go get that beacon.'
One hour later he made it to the beacon. Suddenly, he noticed something shivering. It was the Erser. Swiftly, he turned round and stopped it. It smelt his fear. It took a minute for a fight to break out with the Erser fighting the cadet. The sides were tipping and with one final blow, the Erser was dead.

Oliver Ludkin (8)
Cherhill CE Primary School, Calne

Kangaroos And Robots

One summer's day, in a little hole by Ayres Rock, there lived two kangaroos called Hazel and Nut. It was 5pm when all of a sudden, the wind picked up.
'I don't like it when it's dark,' whispered Nut. You see, Nut was very squeamish, unlike Hazel who was kind and helpful. Just then, an army of mean robots came drilling, bashing into the ground.
'Stop!' screamed Hazel.
'We will destroy your home!' shouted the robots. 'You will just have to move house,' they all shouted.
Just then a massive tornado pushed the robots away.
'Yes!' exclaimed Nut. 'Let's stay.'

Rowan Sabin
Cherhill CE Primary School, Calne

Untitled

One morning, Nala, Edwardo and I went for a walk. I threw Nala's ball. She went running for it. Unfortunately, it went in the bush. Nala still went for it. When I called her name she did not come. She was lost. Edwardo started crying. I told him not to worry, we would soon find her. So I searched in the bush.
One hour later we found her. She was with a boy pug called Buzz. They both loved each other. We did not know who Buzz belonged to. He looked lost then I found his owner. Buzz and Nala kissed.

Abi Jordan (9)
Cherhill CE Primary School, Calne

The Secret Underwater Kingdom

Once upon a time there lived some mermaids who roamed in an underwater kingdom. The mermaids were called Lily, Emma, Ella and Poppy. They were all friends. Suddenly, one day the starfish, Bob and Kate had bad news. 'Pirates are coming. They're going to invade,' shouted the starfish.
A few hours later, the pirates came but two girls called Alice and Meghan came. They got an army of sharks to kill and scare away the pirates. When the girls found out that Meghan and Alice saved the day, they said, 'Thank you.' They all started becoming really good friends.

Bethan Evans (9)
Cherhill CE Primary School, Calne

The Greek Fantastic Future Footballers And Geoff

Once upon a time there were six Greek footballers called Holebas, Papadopoulos, Kostanios, Mitroglou, Samaras and Samaris. Their manager was called Geoff.
The next day they were playing a match against Poland. After 60 minutes playing, they had a fight and out of nowhere, Geoff was kidnapped. So the six footballers went on a mission to save Geoff. They got to the place and they were disguised as the guards. They were following the other guards. They finally found Geoff and sneaked away, so they lived a happy life forever.

George William Charles Wilcox (9)
Cherhill CE Primary School, Calne

Fireland

Long, long ago, fire was everywhere. Meanwhile, fire animals developed. Dangerous animals like fire birds and fire goblins. Next, fire knights, also fire armies. Luckily, fire fighters were there as well. They were at war. The naughty goblin tried to shoot them but he was caught. Suddenly, a lava tidal wave came and killed 200 people. Soon, fire fighters put out the fire and then they built 2,000 buildings and animals. The animals turned into people and the rest of the people died. Soon, more people lived and designed maths and writing, also books. Eventually, the dangerous animals became tame.

Digby King (8)
Cherhill CE Primary School, Calne

The Evil Pencil

One cold, rainy day, Bob the evil pencil was in his secret den. There was a kind, pretty girl called Lily. She had heard about Bob and that he wanted to destroy the world! He only wanted to end the world because he could not get what he wanted. His parents died when he was little, so he was very lonely. Suddenly, Bob got a massive sharpener and started sharpening the world! Luckily, Lily brought Bob's parents back so he would stop destroying the world. Lily used her powers to bring Bob's parents back and fix the world.

Lily Godwin (9)
Cherhill CE Primary School, Calne

It's A Hard Life For Ellie

One day there was a family. There was a mum, dad and daughter. The daughter was called Ellie, the mum was called Lia and the dad was called Michael. They were a happy family until now. When Ellie started school there were three mean boys, their names were Elliot, Jude and Harry. Their nickname was 'The Mean Boys'. They were being mean ever since Ellie started school. Lia got really mad when Ellie came home crying because of the mean boys so Michael decided to stop it all as he was the headmaster. Now they are a happy family again.

Lily Matthieson (8)
Cherhill CE Primary School, Calne

Bobby And The Magical Marshmallow

Once upon a time, Bobby was running down the path until he noticed something extremely strange. The weird thing was he could hear strange noises behind the wall, so using his laser gun he zapped a hole in the wall. The machine said 'Grude and Dr Moody'. It was a marshmallow gun. Bobby jumped down holding his laser gun in his hand. Dr Moody muttered, 'We're trapped!' but then Grude fired the marshmallow gun at Bobby but suddenly, it shot back at Dr Moody and Grude! Then a flying cow came out of nowhere and gobbled them up.

Theo Anderson (9)
Cherhill CE Primary School, Calne

Fairy Finder

One day, a little girl called Betty sat on her sofa to watch telly. But, suddenly, she mysteriously got sucked into her sofa! Betty got dropped into a white, airy room. At that moment, a fairy came along, tinkling her wings. She led Betty into a black, misty tunnel. Soon, she got out of the tunnel...
Betty saw mushroom houses and cute fairies fluttering about. Betty was in Heaven!
'Betty, come here,' demanded the queen fairy. 'Welcome to your new home, Mushroom Forest. This is Pixi, your tour guide. I hope you girls have fun.'
Betty loved her new home!

Sophie Norris (9)
Cherhill CE Primary School, Calne

At Sea With Bob And Harry The Scientists

In the splashy sea there was a sub and it belonged to Bob the minion and Harry the scientist. One black and gloomy day, Bob was asleep and Harry was testing his robot. Suddenly, the sub went mad. Bob woke up and Harry said, 'There are intruders, Bob! Get the freeze gun.'
Bob went to make the shark and the octopus die. Bob aimed the freeze gun and *poof,* the octopus and shark died. Bob and Harry lived happily ever after.

Harry Bolwell (8)
Cherhill CE Primary School, Calne

The Magic Of Football

One day, Charlie Adams and Asmil were challenged to a match by Harry Kane and Lugo Lloris. As soon as the ball had been kicked off, Adams got the ball. Kane tried to tackle but by the time he got there, Adams lobbed it. It was as if the world had stopped and the ball smashed in. One-nil to Stoke. Tottenham's team was furious. Then they scored an own goal, it was hilarious. 2-0 to Stoke. The full-time whistle blew just as Tottenham tried to score. At full time it was 2-0 to Stoke.

Noah Finney (8)
Cherhill CE Primary School, Calne

Cinderella And The Prince!

One sunny day there lived a beautiful girl named Cinderella. She lived with her stepmother and stepsisters.
One day, a letter appeared at their front door from Prince Charming about a ball. But Cinderella wasn't allowed to go because she had lots to do at home.
When it was time to go, Cinderella's stepmother locked her in a big tower and she couldn't get out. Cinderella needed to be saved by Prince Charming. When he went past the tower, he didn't realise she was in there. Suddenly, she called out to Prince Charming and he came to save her.

Amelia Haley (9)
Cherhill CE Primary School, Calne

Fish And Mermaids

There was an underwater sea and there was a mermaid called Sofia and lots of fish. She found a magical place. She was amazed how pretty it was. She couldn't pick up all of the treasure, then she went and got her family. She grabbed her mum and swam to the treasure. Sofia and her family were really happy. They were rich! They celebrated by moving house and for the rest of her life, Sofia had fun! She was so happy!

Lully Lavis (7)
Cherhill CE Primary School, Calne

Swindon V Tottenham

One day there were three friends and they all played for Swindon. But one evening there was a game on. Swindon were playing Tottenham but when they saw a player for Tottenham called Harry Kane, the Swindon players were feeling scared. Then Foderingham, Gladwin and Thompson met Harry Kane and the game started. Gladwin scored for Swindon Town. But then Tottenham had a penalty because Thompson found Harry Kane in the penalty box. Foderingham saved it and kept it. 1-0 still. Then Swindon scored again. It was Gladwin and then the game finished and Foderingham and Thompson went home.

Rhys Simpkins (8)
Cherhill CE Primary School, Calne

Snow White And Rose Red

Snow White was riding in a golden carriage with her prince. Suddenly, they came to a stop. Snow White got out and saw her sister, Rose Red. Snow White's sister screamed, 'What are you doing?' Rose Red was identical to Snow White but with blood-red hair.
Snow White said, 'Sorry.' She got back into the carriage and went to the castle. Rose Red started to cry. She ran after her sister but the carriage was too fast. When she finally reached the shiny castle, she was too late, Snow White was already getting married to the prince.

Imogen Burks (7)
Cherhill CE Primary School, Calne

Sammy's Brick House

Once upon a time, there was a family of four pigs, three piglets and a mummy pig. One day, Mummy Pig said to Sammy, James and Jack, 'Go now. Build your own houses.'
'OK!' they all shouted.
James built his house out of straw and Jack built his house out of sticks. But Sammy very cleverly built his out of bricks. Suddenly, the wolf came and blew the other two houses down! Sammy's stayed the same. Sammy lent his left-over bricks to his brothers to build a new home. 'Thanks!' they said.

Milly Howes (9)
Cherhill CE Primary School, Calne

Prince Harp Saves Polly

Polly was a really nice girl but her parents died, so her stepsisters (who were ugly and mean) had to look after her. They were called Jane and Pitty. They said that Polly was not allowed out to play. She asked, 'Please, Jane and Pitty, I want to go out to play. It's not fair.'
Pitty answered, 'You are not going out to play.'
So she went upstairs and into her room. She looked out the window. There was Prince Harp there. He went in and saved her. Then they went to the castle and got cakes and drinks.

Kayleigh Weston-Blake (9)
Cherhill CE Primary School, Calne

The Storm...

There was a man called Wes. He was just playing a football match when the wind started to pick up. It got very cloudy and then it was raining golf balls! Suddenly, a tornado appeared. It had just touched down at Swindon Stadium when it went away. Wes was very hurt but then the winds got stronger again. It was just the eye of the storm. The winds were becoming dangerous. Then the tornado had gone. Lots of people were very hurt and it destroyed Swindon Town and the rest of Swindon. It was very scary! Wes was very hurt.

Freddie Smith (8)
Cherhill CE Primary School, Calne

Lily's Life

Once upon a time there was a little girl who lived up a magic tree and never came down. Her name was Lily. One day, she fell out the tree. She was very angry. So was the tree because it was magic. When Lily fell, a man was walking along. He had a very long nose and he poked Lily in the eye! 'Ouch!' Lily said.
Then the man gave her a drink but it was poison, which made her fall in love with him. Lily started to drink and then fell in love straight away. Then they got married.

Daisy Winstone (8)
Cherhill CE Primary School, Calne

Horses Escape

There were horses who broke the fence because they didn't like their owner. It was quite hard to break the fence. When the owner saw what had happened, she was upset. The horses ran so fast, they were at the river. They jumped the river and came to a field full of grass. They ate lots of grass and they were soon tired so they tried to find their way home. It took all night to get home. Their owner was so happy, she rode Chance, her favourite horse. Then she rode all of them!

Olivia Gibbs-Perutz (8)
Cherhill CE Primary School, Calne

Untitled

One day there was a boy called Isaac. He randomly stepped on a button and teleported to the Ice Age. He looked and looked for a way back home, but he couldn't find one.
One day, he heard a noise. It was a sabre-toothed tiger and some woolly mammoths. He ran and ran and ran screaming, 'Mummy!' Then he hid in a cave and waited. Later, he came out of the cave but suddenly he got ambushed and got gobbled up by the king sabre-toothed tiger!

Jake Floyd (9)
Cherhill CE Primary School, Calne

Maney And The Missing Diamond

Suddenly, the alarm screeched! Maney wanted to know what it was, so he asked the computer. He said Dr Porkchop was trying to follow them to find the diamond.
'Turn on the invisibility cloak,' yelled Maney.
'OK, master!'
Suddenly, they disappeared. 'Where did they go?' asked Dr Porchop angrily.
'We've reached the moon!' shouted Maney. So they parked their spaceship. Then they put their moon clothes on and set off. Unfortunately, they found nothing. Then the computer cried out, 'I've found the diamond!'
Suddenly, everyone raced over. 'Hooray!' they yelled and drove back home happily.

Freya Rowe (8)
Cherhill CE Primary School, Calne

The Switch Of Snow White

Once, many years ago, there was an evil queen who lived in a dark castle. In the forest, the seven dwarfs lived in a cottage with Snow White. One day, the queen came and knocked on the cottage door and offered Snow White an apple. The queen had two apples, one to make herself extra evil and more powerful and one to make Snow White extra good. But it was the wrong one! That night they both went to bed. When they woke up, Snow White was evil, the evil queen had turned good. Snow White killed the seven dwarfs!

Evie Grace Carter (9)
Cherhill CE Primary School, Calne

Little Red Riding Hood

One day, Red Riding Hood went into the magic forests. Suddenly, she saw Jack and Jill gardening. Then there was a cheeky, naughty and hairy wolf. It was the big bad wolf! He took Jill to his secret hideout where he ate people for dinner. Red Riding Hood and Jack raced to stop the wolf. The wolf was trying to block them. 'Stop, you big meanie!' But then the wolf started to cry. Jill asked the big bad wolf if he wanted to be friends. The wolf said yes and they all played nicely. They all lived happily ever after.

Grace Perrett (9)
Cherhill CE Primary School, Calne

Fish To The Rescue!

One day under the sea, the magic pearl was stolen. So Mr Fish, Miss Fish and Baby Fish went to get the pearl. On their way, they went past magic caves that looked spooky because they had some eyes in them. Then they came to a bridge. They swam over the top of it. Then they found the pearl but it was guarded by fish ninjas. Mr Fish said, 'Let's get them.' Then they got the strength food and killed the fish ninjas. They had to kill the boss. Then they got the pearl and went back home.

Lexie House (9)
Cherhill CE Primary School, Calne

Best Buddies Forever

Once, there was a dolphin and a seahorse. The seahorse was called Lilly and the dolphin was called Sally. They were best buddies since they were pups.

One day, they were playing and Sally had to find Lilly. 'There you are,' said Sally and got ready to dash through the rocks. 'One, two, go!' Oh no! Just then, Sally got her tail stuck.

Later, Lilly took her to Clamy the nurse who said, 'Look after her and she will be OK.'

So Lilly looked after her for a month until she was OK.

Emma Egan (9)
Cherhill CE Primary School, Calne

Football

Once upon a time there were four footballers called Messi, Ronaldo, Sanchez and Swarez. One day it was Arsenal versus Real Madrid. When it started, Sanchez was feeling very worried that his team might lose. Arsenal started the match and scored one goal in the first minute. They were in the second half and it was 2-1 to Arsenal. When the game ended, Sanchez, Ronaldo, Messi and Swarez went to McDonald's and had a cheeseburger each. They had a chat then went home on their posh motorbikes and got stuck in traffic.

Isaac Covington (8)
Cherhill CE Primary School, Calne

The Fire On Mars

Doggy, Baby and Mummy were inside their huge spaceship flying to Mars. Doggy was excited. Then Mummy cried, 'Argh!' Baby and Doggy were worried, they looked out of one of the huge glass windows. On Mars there was a flaming fire. Mummy steered the ship and landed on a non-flaming area of Mars. They walked slowly towards the flames. Mummy and Doggy had left Baby in the fireproof ship. It was getting worse! Doggy had an idea. Quickly, he ran back to the ship. He came back with a fire engine. He turned on the hose and squirted out the fire!

Rhiannon Moth (9)
Cherhill CE Primary School, Calne

The Fall Out

Once there were five friends: Tinkerbell, Olaf, Peter Pan, Woody and Jessy. They all shared a house. One day, Olaf threw a snowball at Tink's hair and then her clip fell in Woody's soup. He chucked the soup into Jessy's hat. Jessy chucked her hat in Peter's eye. 'Olaf!' shouted the group. They all shouted at each other. 'Guys, stop! Look, we can be friends if we want to,' said Peter. 'Peter's right,' they all said. They all said sorry to each other and celebrated with a pizza night like they used to. They still have pizza night today!

Emmie Lynch (9)
Cherhill CE Primary School, Calne

Untitled

One sunny day, there was a footballer called Ronaldo and he got the best goal ever. An academy picked him up and it was called Real Madrid. It was his dream. He was the best.

It was his first match. It was against FC Barcelona. The game had started. Ronaldo's manager was pleased with him. He'd already had some three shots on target already. At half-time it was a tie. It was a close match. Real Madrid had a penalty and Ronaldo scored. They had now won the match.

Bill Marsh (8)
Cherhill CE Primary School, Calne

The Lonely Horse

Years ago there was a horse called Samson. He was abandoned on a deserted island called the Island of Death. This island was covered with poison ivy and he'd never eaten any before. As night fell, he was alone, no one to feed him or ride him.

In the morning, a boat came along and loaded Samson onto the ship. It sailed away off into the distance. When they came to the Land of Unicorns, they all got off the ship and got a drink from the River Nile. They were all refreshed after that. They hopped back in and sailed away.

Bodie Sinnick (10)
Cherhill CE Primary School, Calne

The Magic Stone!

Mimi was walking through the treetops when all of a sudden, the tribe's emergency call went off. The tribe leader, Joe, had found something. Everyone raced to the main tree house. When Mimi reached the tree house, her parents were waiting. Joe had found a magic stone. Because it was smooth and shiny, everyone touched it. Joe explained where he'd found it.

In the morning, they were all animals. They knew how to turn back into humans, but then found the tribe of leopards had destroyed what they needed to turn back. Would they ever be humans again?

Sophie McIntyre (11)
Cherhill CE Primary School, Calne

The Unwanted Place

My name is Annabel, I'm 13 and this is my diary. I was there, the most unwanted place to be, Haunted Stables! You're probably wondering why I'm here. It's because it was a donkey dare. This reluctant place had been cursed ever since Friday 13th, 1939. It was surrounded by wrecked trees, leaning over as if they were going to crush me. I walked in. I saw a body, a dead body! I carried on, unsure what was going to happen next. Suddenly, out of the blue, I saw bones, horse bones! This is surely haunted. Will this remain forever?

Molly Burton (11)
Cherhill CE Primary School, Calne

Underwater Discovery

Hi, I'm Oliver Gregg, I'm 22 and I'm a diver. I've made a brand new discovery like no other. Now this is how I found it. I was at the beach doing what I please, doing my job, just diving. It might sound boring, but then I touched something. I couldn't see it, it was invisible so I went back up to get more kit to survive the dangerous creatures inside, but there were only portals inside. I stepped inside one but it appeared to send me 65 million years ago. Suddenly, a T-rex went to eat me. I survived.

Max John Dore-Wright (10)
Cherhill CE Primary School, Calne

Space Mission

I'm in space, my first mission is to find a new planet to live on before the Earth explodes! All the planets look amazing but my sensor says the air is toxic. I go check on the oxygen supply but before I get there, I hear a beeping noise. *It is the oxygen.* They must have forgotten to refill it. I have to go back, but this is too far away. I have to keep on going! There in front of me is the planet I have been looking for. I'm gasping for air...
I've made it! The perfect planet.

Oliver Graham (10)
Cherhill CE Primary School, Calne

The Destroyed Island!

Years ago there was a man called Guy Forks. He had black hair, a beard and he was also very old and grey. His crew included 20 men. He loved his crew and didn't want them to die because of the enemies. When he went to lie on the beach with the rest of his crew, he saw a ship. When it got closer, bullets came out of the front of it. By the time the ship came to shore, everybody was dead, even the amazing captain, Guy Forks.

Aleana Edwards (9)
Cherhill CE Primary School, Calne

The Dream

When I woke up this morning, I was very excited because it was my birthday! I quickly ran and my family was waiting for me with my presents. There were four big and two small ones. I opened them. I got two cages, two boxes with stuff to go in the cages, green mambas. My dream had come true. Just then, I woke up. 'Argh! It was just a dream!'

Warren Muggeridge (10)
Cherhill CE Primary School, Calne

One Step Ahead

Discovering the ancient mammoth is an honour. I can't believe that the almighty mammoth will be in combat with me. We are off to Dr Gangformer's lab in North America. Feeling confident until... I see Dr Gangformer and the master of destruction, the king of all animals, the T-rex! Charging towards Dr Gangformer and his T-rex is nerve-wracking. I'm petrified. We carry on. The gigantic T-rex is taller than 15 double decker buses on top of each other. The T-rex grabs me by the waist, roars with all his might! I'm trying to escape but the force is too strong.

Amelia Frances Ann Lambourne (10)
Cherhill CE Primary School, Calne

The Cabin In The Woods

John needed a place to sleep, so he wandered carelessly into the very, very creepy wood. There he saw a creepy cabin. Whilst he was getting ready for bed, he noticed there were 12 'paintings'. He thought nothing of it until he woke up. Then he saw the 12 'paintings' had vanished mysteriously. Suddenly, the radio blared. It said, 'Last night 12 mental people escaped from the mental hospital. We advise you to stay indoors.' But John didn't. He wanted to run home so badly, and that's what he did. He ran all the way to his hospital.

Tegan Seed (11)
Cherhill CE Primary School, Calne

The Worst Thing About My Parents

'Mum, Dad, why can't I have a sleepover?' said Lauren, whining.
Dad replied, 'Because of all the glitter and talking about boys all night.'
'But Dad, they're asking me things,' said Lauren.
'What are they asking?' said Mum.
'Like why I haven't had a sleepover yet!' said Lauren, about to cry.
Her dad gave in and said, 'Fine, you can have a sleepover but no glitter!'
'Yay!' said Lauren.
Her friend knocked on the door. Lauren said, 'Guess what? I am having a sleepover!'
'Guess what? I hate sleepovers!' said Hayden.
Lauren said, 'I wasn't looking for that, so unfair!'

Erin Macauley (10)
Cherhill CE Primary School, Calne

Marcus Aurelius' Adventures

My name is Marcus Aurelius. I lead the armies of the north. The Scottish attacked our camp and I was the last one alive. I escaped the battlefield but two days later, they found me and made me into a slave. I needed to do everything for them: cook, wash, clean and worst of all, clean them! Whenever I did something wrong, I would get whipped. I didn't want to live anymore so I started doing everything wrong so they kept punishing me with brutal force. I was put with the alligator in the lake and I died there.

Ethan Rickett (10)
Cherhill CE Primary School, Calne

Ellie And Her Favourite Blanky

There lived a small elephant called Ellie in a big tree house rushing around messing up the house. Everything was scattered everywhere. 'Where is it?' cried Ellie. She was missing her lucky blanky. Ellie went outside.
'Looking for this?' asked one of the tigers, then ran away with it. Ellie tried to catch them but she couldn't. Ellie lay down and cried. She wondered how they got it. Then out of nowhere, Taylor, one of the tigers, gave Ellie her blanky. Taylor and Ellie played. The other tigers watched them play happily, really, really happily.

Eryn Barnes (9)
Cherhill CE Primary School, Calne

Skeleton Invasion

One gloomy night I was in my bed sleeping, when I heard a bang on my door! I woke up scared. I went downstairs to see my dogs but they weren't there! Where were they? I saw something moving out in the back garden. I crept closer to the door I started to see moving bones, it was a skeleton! I went outside to see if it was a skeleton, it was! It hit me then I hit it back, it fell to a pile of bones. Then my dogs appeared! They each grabbed a bone and ran indoors.

Tom Robert Steward (9)
Gretton Primary School, Cheltenham

Misty's Brave Father

Misty was a mermaid. She was happily swimming in the enchanted mermaid village's crystal-clear water, when she sensed something wasn't quite right. As she approached the corner there was a trail of destruction ahead. A colossal sea monster with twenty eyes and sharp scales was chewing up the village like he'd never eaten before! Luckily, Misty's father, Ivan, saw the sea monster and a battle commenced. Ivan's magic staff blasted the sea monster with lava jets which made the monster stop eating and fall to the floor in pain. They stood over the sea monster, but was he dead?

Allayna Skye Pearson (8)
Gretton Primary School, Cheltenham

Untitled

One dark damp day, Leo was training to be a warrior when he saw a horrible lord with scorching red eyes. On Monday someone burned down his house and he was so angry. His friend knew that the lord had done it and knew where he lived. Leo asked a wizard to make a poison potion that looked and tasted like Coke. The lord loved Coke. Leo went to visit the lord, Leo put it in a package, knocked on the door, placed it on the floor and hid. The lord came out, he drank it and died instantly!

Caleb Hammond (7)
Gretton Primary School, Cheltenham

The Invaders

One dark rainy day Percy woke up from his damp wet bed and jumped up and saw dots on the horizon. He thought someone was coming to give them food or more bricks. Then when the mist went away he saw a dragon's head, it stopped. Suddenly he heard a roaring noise, he saw warriors running around like headless chickens destroying everything. People ran away and suddenly flaming arrows burnt down the monastery. A gruesome river of blood travelled slowly down to the horizon, the sea turned red. His father died with blood dripping.

Theo Jones (9)
Gretton Primary School, Cheltenham

The Lost Dog

'Help, Cookie has gone!' Hale screeched, just at the moment she saw her dog vanish! Hale loved her dog so much, but now she was gone! She put her tatty old hat on her blonde wavy hair and set off. Hale zoomed in her new car, and was there in no time. As soon as she stepped in, Badasher was locking Cookie in a trap. 'No way!' Hale accidently shouted. Badasher heard her. How could she possibly survive this? Badasher saw Hale and started fighting, but Badasher splashed her and the dog, so they would be his awful slaves forever!

Emma Whales (9)
Gretton Primary School, Cheltenham

Untitled

'We need to kill that Joker,' shouted Hulk. 'I need to get to the spaceship.'
'What about my rocket?'
The spaceship was enormous. They got out of the rocket. Hawker shot a bow and arrow and it hit the Joker on the head, as quick as a flash Iron Man knocked him over. Hulk did a Hulk smash. Cat Woman whizzed to get the glittering crown. Then they raced out of the spaceship, but Iron Man shot a final missile and the enormous spaceship and all of the people went down, down, down.

Fred Fowler
Gretton Primary School, Cheltenham

The Lost Friend

'She's gone!' shouted Rarity.
'Who's gone?' asked Sunset, groaning as she got up.
'Shimmer!'
'We need to go and find her then, don't we?'
Running towards the horizon, Rarity shouted, 'Where do you think she'll be?'
'I don't know, let's check the hideout first.'
When Rarity and Sunset got to their hideout they couldn't see Shimmer there, so Rarity said, 'Why don't we check our hangout, surely she'll be there.'
A couple of hours later, they arrived at the hangout. They looked everywhere but still Shimmer couldn't be found. 'Quick, follow me. There she is! Shimmer where did you go?'

Harriet
Gretton Primary School, Cheltenham

Funny French Revolution

The queen was mostly famous for cake. The French people were very poor so they raided the queen's house. The poor French people looked for all the cake they could find until there was nothing left. The queen, who was incredibly fat, grew very thin until one day the queen began to starve. All the queen ever ate was cake, cake for breakfast, cake for lunch and cake for dinner. The queen thought what she could do. She didn't sleep until she could make something tasty. Then one day it came to her. She made biscuits. Isn't the queen clever?

Benji Mc
Gretton Primary School, Cheltenham

Max's Space Adventure

'Where is it?' screamed Mum. 'If we don't find them we can't go on our space trip.'
Suddenly Max, the older brother, shouted, 'Found it!' Everyone sprinted into the room. Max handed out the tickets.
Two hours later they were on their way to space. Suddenly something hit them! Max's family thought they would fall forever, but they weren't falling at all. They had landed on a planet in the middle of nowhere. They opened the hatch and tried to walk on the strange new planet. Then suddenly they realised that their dad was not with them. Where was he?

Daniel Hammond (8)
Gretton Primary School, Cheltenham

The Crying Girl

Franky had just moved into her new house, she wanted to explore so she walked outside. A tree at the end of the garden caught Franky's eye. She walked up to the tree, she touched the tree. Then she disappeared. She found herself in the tree. 'Argh!' screamed Franky. She could hear crying, she followed the sound. A few minutes later, she found a girl who was crying. 'Are you OK?' asked Franky.
'Yes, I'm just very upset because nobody has time for me.'
The girl and Franky became the best of friends.

Megan Jayne Bray (9)
Gretton Primary School, Cheltenham

Three Little Mermaids

'Oh no, Lilly's gone!' shouted Milly. 'We have to go and rescue her. We have to bring the friendly monster too and also bring the cookies in case we get hungry.' So they set off and in the sea was the sea monster. The sea monster locked the mermaids in a cage in the prison. The friendly sea monster saw the sea monster sleeping so the friendly sea monster got the mermaids out of their cage and they swam away until they saw another sea monster. It swam away.

Ava Bawdon (7)
Gretton Primary School, Cheltenham

Fuchsia And The Secret Forest

A dog called Fuchsia dug a hole in the garden. I went in the hole with her, we came out in a magical forest where a Pegasus pony called Rainbow Dash led us to a tree house which we used as a secret house that Pegasus ponies guarded.

One day Rainbow Dash said to me and Fuchsia that a dragon tried to burn the tree house down. He kept breathing fire but it would not burn because the unicorn pony who lived there before cast a spell so no danger could harm the house. The tree house lived on forever.

Jessica Drew (10)
Huntley CE Primary School, Gloucester

Final Iron Man!

Once upon a time there it was - final Iron Man. He met a green woman, she was evil and crazy. Iron Man knew everything, he went into her lab. Then it started! The green evil lady came. Iron Man did an amazing slide tackle. Iron Man flew home, what a night. The curtains blew, the kettle was going off, it was scary. Iron Man couldn't cope. He went to fight again. The green lady planned something, she jumped at Iron Man, he jumped back. The green crazy lady couldn't stand it so gave up, then she was gone.

Hannah York (8)
Huntley CE Primary School, Gloucester

T-Rex Treck And Friends - The Erupting Volcano

One day, on Dino Island, 'Oh no, a volcano is erupting!' screeched T-rex Treck and Raptor.
Robbie said, 'What are we going to do Treck?'
'Look, there's Hybrid and his minions!' screamed Dino Dan.
'You will never stop me and I made the volcano erupt!'
'Let's get to work Dino Team!' *Pow*! *Wham*! *Smack*!
'Dino Dan, throw that boulder in the hole in the volcano!' shouted T-rex Treck.
'Noooooooooo!' howled Hybrid.
'Get them, minions, now!'
'Dino Dan, punch Hybrid into the universe!' said T-rex Treck.
'OK, let's do this thing!' said Dino Dan.
Pow! 'Yeah!' shouted everybody.

James Collins (9)
Huntley CE Primary School, Gloucester

Avatar

One night a boy found his inner power to become the Avatar. He went to the Water Nation to get Katara to teach him water bending and he went to the Earth Kingdom to learn earth bending. Then he had to meet his worst fear - fire bending. In time he mastered it. So, he went on his way to defeat the army. When he faced the Fire Lord he used all his powers to defeat him. As a reward, his friends took him to the moon with their powers. Afterwards, he dropped his friends off and went home safely.

Jacob Daniel Atkinson (9)
Huntley CE Primary School, Gloucester

Magic Loop!

One evening, Princess Venice awoke to find Night Ed, her future husband, with his friend Night Than. He looked at Princess Venice and he cried out loud, 'We shall be married in the morning, tomorrow!'
Princess Venice announced in the evening, 'There is going to be a marriage.'
Because Night Ed knew about this he said, 'Goodbye,' to Princess Venice. At the end of the wedding he gave her a special wedding gift and it was special alright. It was a sparkling special pink, blue, green, red, yellow, purple, spotty, striped, brilliant egg! It was so very cool.

Libbi Justice (9)
Huntley CE Primary School, Gloucester

The Abandoned Shack!

It was cold, Alex was lost! He had been wandering for hours, lost for eternity. Suddenly, he spotted a little shack in the distance! Alex ran towards it in relief. As he entered he felt an ice-cold shiver run down his spine. Rot and decay lined the walls and the floorboards creaked with each step Alex took! All of a sudden, there was an almighty flash of lightning! There in the doorway stood a terrifying sight. A shadowy figure stood there silently watching Alex's every move! Then it struck him! This was the day he'd finally meet his fate!

Jazzy Saunders (10)
Huntley CE Primary School, Gloucester

Mates Save The Day

One day, Superman and Spider-Man were in the town when they got a message, 'Help us, we are trapped in Loki's lair.' So Superman and Spider-Man went to save Ross and Robbin. 'Yes, we're in. Argh! Frost giants! Let's attack... that was so easy, now let's save Ross and Robbin.'
'Help! Help!'
'There they are.'
'Spider-Man, not so fast!' Loki shouts, 'Marvel's heroes, I've got your friends, unless you want to fight?'
'OK.' So Spider-Man and Superman fought until they got bored, but in the fight Superman saved Ross and Robbin and they went back to the town.

Fin Rawlings (9)
Huntley CE Primary School, Gloucester

The Spoilt Princess

Once there was a girl called Ella-Mae, her mother treated her as a princess and bought her diamond tiaras, she was very spoilt. One day her mother sent her to boarding school, Ella-Mae thought she was going to Princess Academy but she was going to a little school. She got out of the car and went in. She saw everyone, their names were: Jenny, Rebecca, Alex and Danny. 'Grow up princess,' they all shouted. Ella-Mae felt very upset. They kept calling her names, like 'goody-goody little princess'. She decided that she wouldn't act like a princess again. Thank goodness!

Jaime-May Meadows (10)
Huntley CE Primary School, Gloucester

The Mystery Cave

'Yes!' cheered Zara, punching the air. She glanced down at the mountain, which she had just quickly walked up towards a mossy cave, the painful thoughts of the painful climb flooding her mind. Cautiously making her way to the entrance, Zara considered if she should have made the effort just to see a cave. Taking one silent step forward, Zara came face to face with something horrid. Cracked. Ugly. Deformed. A face. Small, black, beady eyes pierced through the mist. Tumbling down the hill, Zara sprinted through the forceful rain, shivering, shivering, shivering, shivering with fright.

Holly Jayne Elizabeth Miller (12)
Lulworth & Winfrith CE (VC) Primary School, Wareham

Swimming Starbuck

Once upon a time, there was a small white deer named Starbuck, who loved to dance by the river. This was his favourite thing to do in the whole of Fairytale Land.

One day he saw the otters swimming in the magic, sparkling river, which ran through Fairytale Land. *I wish I could swim*, he thought. Suddenly, a magical doe, with blue flowers on her head, approached. 'I will grant that wish,' she said, as she swished her head and stomped a foot. Starbuck leapt excitedly in the river and began to swim.

Fred Mabey (10)
Lulworth & Winfrith CE (VC) Primary School, Wareham

House Of Death

I stood, stared and wondered, at the old and desolate, smashed and abandoned shack, in the bleak, black wood. I looked in wonder at the wooden door, the same words going round my head like a broken record. *Open the door! Open the door! Open the door!* The broken and smashed windows rose my heart into my throat. Roping vines climbed up the house, like a monkey climbing a tree.

Then I heard a deep and menacing voice calling out. 'Open the door, Billy! Open the door!' Possessed by the house's deathly speech, I opened the door, walking into death.

Billy Winch
Lulworth & Winfrith CE (VC) Primary School, Wareham

The Magical Crystal Part 1

Once upon a time, a young girl named Sasha was on a mission to find her grandmother's magical crystal that had been in her family for centuries. She walked out of the old brick castle and her dog trotted along too, Truffles went into the forbidden corner of the mysterious garden. 'Woof! Woof!'
'What is it Truffles?' And there lay a piece of paper. 'A riddle,' announced Sasha. She read with confidence, Sasha energetically jumped over the fence and there it was! She'd found it! She clutched it in her fist, it was hers at last!...

Chloe Freeman (10)
Lulworth & Winfrith CE (VC) Primary School, Wareham

Footballing Monkeys

Far away in a world full of monkeys, Jim and Bob were munching on marvellous bananas. 'Jim it's time to go,' Mother told Jim.
'See you tomorrow at the big game,' Bob nudged Jim.
'Will do,' Jim replied.
Jim strolled on home. They both got tucked up in bed.
Nice and early in the morning they both met at the football pitch. The first half, they scored one and so did the other team. However, in the second half, Jim and Bob both scored two each. In the end they won 5-1. They won the cup and celebrated all night.

Eva Neat (10)
Lulworth & Winfrith CE (VC) Primary School, Wareham

The Last Day

Bang! *Bang*! went the guns. 'Help!' cried a girl. 'Help me!' *Bang*! The last thing went down. 'Thank you, what's your name?' 'John,' said the man, 'now let's get out of this place.' As they were running down the alley a roar came from a house. A massive thing came out of the house. John pulled the trigger but he was out of ammo. The thing came closer...

Kieran Eite (11)
Lulworth & Winfrith CE (VC) Primary School, Wareham

Destroyers

In the time of 2335, the world was under attack. *Bang*! 'Look out,' yelled Bob.
'God help us, we are running out of time and ammo,' yelled James. There they were on the streets of New York with aliens closing in on them.
'Why did this happen on Christmas,' said Angel Sam. They ran and hid in a chocolate shop, the reason was because it was sweet. *Bang*! came a blast through the door. There he was, Commander Azale, leader of the Earth slavery camp.
'Surrender or be destroyed,' announced Azale. He marched them out, all except Stoe...

James Allan (11)
Lulworth & Winfrith CE (VC) Primary School, Wareham

The English Panda

Hello there, my name is Greg, I'm a panda and I live in the Kiingourgo Forest, but it's really boring here. So tomorrow I head to England.
Phew! I finally made it, but all the swimming was really hard. On the lighter side, I've bought a ticket to go on the London Eye.
I'm dizzy, Oh my, those guards have unusual hair and that building is superb. The walls aren't that big. That was easy, what's the old lady with the gold thingy on her head saying? It sounds like, off with his head!

Oscar Dale (11)
Lulworth & Winfrith CE (VC) Primary School, Wareham

My Puppy

I've always wanted a puppy. One day Mum said, 'If you are good, we can get a puppy.'
Of course I said, 'Yes.'
Our friends said that they had puppies for sale and we replied, 'Yes, please.' We found a black puppy we liked, with a white flash down her tummy. We called her Ebony. Ebony was very excited when we first met her. Her floppy ears and wet nose made her very cute. She is coming home next week. I am so excited.

Ben Warren (9)
Ramsbury Primary School, Marlborough

Tom And The Pained Crab

Once, there was a puppy called Tom. He had a thoughtful, lovely owner, who was called Livy. Livy was walking Tom on a nice sunny day, along the canal. She started throwing big and little sticks for him. Eventually, Livy threw a twig into the canal and Tom furiously ran to get it. There was a great splash when he launched into the water. Tom went to fetch the twig, he couldn't find it. Tom kept on sinking down, down and down. He saw a crab leaping with pain. 'What's the matter?' said Tom.
'Come here and see...'

Jessie Strover (8)
Ramsbury Primary School, Marlborough

The Bloodhounds

It was a dark night in Cranium, the soldiers were ready, a black evil was coming. They were called The Bloodhounds, the clue's in the name and today was the big day. Death King was the leader of The Bloodhounds. They started with a death wave, killing the villagers, after they went to face the soldiers. They broke the battle lines and headed for the castle. When they got there they found the Arkomrack. 'Grab it,' Soul said, 'and let's get out of here.' They jumped past the guards.
'Mwhahaha,' Aragon said, 'it is time for evolution!'

George Marren (9)
Ramsbury Primary School, Marlborough

Ferocious Fowey!

We left on our boat to Fowey for a super expensive holiday, when we were attacked by a sea monster and it ate my auntie. At least, I thought it did. It sort of swished her around and spat her out. Luckily, it spat her out onto the shore because she cannot swim. We suddenly sped away at about 1,000 miles per hour because we didn't want to get eaten. We soon arrived at our strange new house with our awesome, private estuary. We had a look around and went crabbing, we even saw a wild dolphin at the harbour!

Pj Gregory (9)
Ramsbury Primary School, Marlborough

The Race

'On your marks, get set, go!' The race has begun. Bob trips up while everyone else is sprinting. Jack fires a catapult at Fred's leg. Jack is disqualified. Oscar and Miles collide and are carried off on stretchers. Oliver's shoe comes off and hits Will in the face. He is out cold. The rest are fighting for first place. In the meantime, Bob is trying to catch up. Tom gets into a fight with Oliver, they are sent off. Who will be the last survivor? Will anyone else get disqualified? They all struggle to the finishing line. Bob is victorious!

Finn Smith (9)
Ramsbury Primary School, Marlborough

Eagle Adventure

One day an eagle was migrating when he entered a thick cloud of fog. He couldn't see and bumped into a mountain.
A couple of days later, he found himself in a cage. Outside of his cage he could see other animals in cages. Then he saw people, he realised he was in a zoo! *Squawk!* Everyone turned in amusement, just then the zookeeper came and opened the cage to feed him but he then flapped his wings and... *whoosh*! He was gone!
A couple of months later, he found his nest and family together in the Himalayas.

Alexander Withington (9)
Ramsbury Primary School, Marlborough

The Pizza Monster

Once, in the early 1960s, there was a restaurant called Perfect Pizza. It was the biggest business in town until the dreaded monster came about...
Strangely, one night, the smallest pizza, which was barely the size of a saucer, disappeared! But Perfect Pizza had loads of pizzas, so it wasn't much of a big deal. Overnight, all the food in stock vanished. Security caught a monster-sized pizza on camera eating the food stock! As the company bought more, the pizza monster ate more. But then the olive came and punched him, very... very... extremely hard. *Bam*! *Bam*!

Eleanor Whitehead (9)
Ramsbury Primary School, Marlborough

The Mermaid And The Princess

Once a princess called Amy came down to the sea. She saw something, she just thought it was a fish. But then it was too big to be a fish. She clambered onto the rocks to see. But then she slipped, tumbling further and further and then she saw a... *mermaid!* Amy didn't hurt herself badly, she only had a little cut. The mermaid cast a spell on the cut, Amy looked down - she was a mermaid. She wanted to repay the mermaid for what she did and all she wished for was a best friend for ever.

Isabella Spreadbury (9)
Ramsbury Primary School, Marlborough

The Biscuit Monster

Once upon a time, there was a girl called Lucy. Yesterday she went to the shops to get some biscuits, for her mum for Mother's Day. Lucy bought some Italian shortbread. When Lucy got home it was very late at night, so she hid the biscuits in her secret drawer. Then she went to bed.
The next morning, Lucy realised that the biscuits had been eaten by a hungry biscuit monster. Lucy explained about the biscuits and her mum said, 'You don't need to give me a present, you only need to give me hug.'

Imogen Orford (9)
Ramsbury Primary School, Marlborough

Just Touch Water

Once, there was a teenage girl. She loved swimming, some people called her a mermaid... One day, she found a pool behind her house, she decided to get in. *Whoosh*! She turned into a mermaid. 'What happened?' she wondered. She decided to get out, maybe it was a dream or something. She went inside, she went to get a drink.

'Emily,' shouted her mum, 'could you help me bath Leon?'

'OK,' she said, 'I will.'

But as soon as she got her hands wet, *whoosh*!

Tatiana E R Waite (9)
Ramsbury Primary School, Marlborough

The Girl In The Picture

The shop was quiet. It was eleven pm. The girl in the picture started to wake up as she did every night. She peered across the shop noticing something unusual, a robber taking items of jewellery and putting them in his bag. The girl panicked and shouted out, 'Thief!' The security guard woke with a fright, and chased the robber towards the door. He caught him and locked him in a cupboard before calling the police! The girl silently moved back into the background of the picture. The security guard still wonders who it was that woke him that evening.

Anya Hodgson (9)
Ramsbury Primary School, Marlborough

Bob The Dog

Bob did not like eating outside. He got too hot, the flies attacked his food, leaves fell on top and dust blew and stuck to his meatballs. Bob liked curling up in his kennel with his big china bowl, containing all of his goodies for the day. He wanted peace and quiet and not to share with anyone or anything. He would start by sniffing, then licking, then nibbling, then munching, then chomping, then gobbling until it was gone. Then he fell asleep, full to the brim, snoring and with his face in his bowl.

Gregie Finn (9)
Ramsbury Primary School, Marlborough

Dangerous Dinosaurs

Teleport woke up, walked slowly (he knew he was late) to the main hall, everyone was sitting waiting. Solid was in the middle of explaining something. 'You finally turned up Teleport, the master of teleportation,' he rolled his eyes, 'anyway as you're here, the Spikeosaurus escaped and we are sending you with drones to stop it.' Teleport nodded. He jumped in a jet and sped off. When he landed, the drones were already there, so was the Spikeosaurus. Teleport grabbed a knife and stabbed it. It fell. 'That was nothing, the adult has awoken,' said Solid, he sighed heavily.

Joshua Walker (9)
Ramsbury Primary School, Marlborough

A Wish Come True

Once there was a girl called Olivia who longed to do ballet. One day her mum said she could, she was so happy she gave her mum a big hug. Olivia jumped in the air with delight. Olivia joined a group of girls in her ballet class, they got on really well. She tried really hard to pick up everything they were doing.
One day her teacher said, 'We're going to do a Hansel and Gretel play.' Olivia practised harder for the play. The night of the play came, when she was on stage, Olivia glittered in the spotlight.

Amie Smart (8)
Ramsbury Primary School, Marlborough

Over Mountain Tops

Malin was a dwarf and one day he decided he would risk his life to travel over the misty mountain tops to find his lost brother. Within hours he set off and reached the Misty Mountains. They towered over him but he continued on. Malin soon realised how lonely the old mountains were as the silence swallowed him whole. Then suddenly it started to get lighter and Malin thought he saw grassy green fields. He walked through the rest of the mountains and the green fields appeared before Malin, and there stood his brother, striding towards him.

Georgie Richardson (10)
St Joseph's Catholic School, Malmesbury

Betty's Adventure

Betty the biscuit was shy and scared of being eaten, but she couldn't bring herself to escape! Whereas Billy wasn't going to get eaten, so he scrambled out with his crumbly legs and body; reluctantly Betty followed. Once they'd escaped the wrapper, Billy pounced off the table, but instead of landing gracefully he fell with a thump onto the floor, shouting, 'Don't be afraid Betty, there is no need!' She scuttled off, terrified, looking behind her at all times. But... oh no, she ran into someone's hand and got eaten. So Betty did have something to be afraid of.

Lucy Cloke (10)
St Joseph's Catholic School, Malmesbury

The Forest's Trap

Once upon a time, in a forest in the heart of Africa, lived three animals, a toucan, macaw, and a monkey. They lived normal animal lives but one day that all changed! It was a beautiful sunny morning and the leaves were glowing like emeralds, the sun was seeping through cracks in the treetops. The monkey spotted this cage; in it were worms. The monkey thought the toucan might like the worms, so he told the toucan to get them. Then the macaw heard a blood-curdling squawk, it was the toucan - he was trapped! How would he get out?

Arthur Wicks (11)
St Joseph's Catholic School, Malmesbury

Death Turns Round!

As Lyra walked along the crumbling road the sun bore down on her. Suddenly a cold feeling of dread began the creep over her like a mad, evil witch! She slumped on the ground in excruciating agony; her breath rapid and chest cold and clammy. She started to panic as the sun sank and darkness swathed her as thick and murky as fog. A hooded figure emerged out of the shadows and spoke! 'I'm Death!' The voice was bleak and mutinous. The darkened charcoal-black face zoomed in closer: *Flash*! And Lyra was launched into everlasting blackness for all eternity!

Noah Halton (10)
St Joseph's Catholic School, Malmesbury

The Marshmallow That Grew Legs

There once lived a marshmallow named Marshall. He grew up in a sweet shop in Dewberry. He had been sad for a while now because his friends had legs, but he didn't! He was so sad, he hated every customer there was. But one day he was so sad the next customer (named Ted, aged 4) that came in, Marshall did something terrible, he ate Ted!
The next day Marshall felt funny, (I wonder why!) It's as if he had grown legs! Lilly the liquorice and Julie the Jelly Bean, were so glad he could walk! And so was Marshall.

Sophie Dickson (11)
St Joseph's Catholic School, Malmesbury

The Earthquake

'I am soooo happy!' shouted Rocky. Rocky and Eggy are going to Awesome Land. When they get there, a massive rumble echoes everywhere, Rocky is petrified! Rocky looks out the window; all the buildings have fallen to their awful end. Suddenly, one of the gigantic buildings falls on the house that Eggy and Rocky are in! They are trapped...
It has been three days since Rocky and Eggy have eaten. Rocky is sooo weak! Eggy with his supreme strength lifts the building and firemen save Rocky! Everyone is happy and no one will go to Awesome Land again!

Raph Rottiers (11)
St Joseph's Catholic School, Malmesbury

The Glazed Hanging Icicle!

On one winter's afternoon a crystallised icicle hung from a shed in a school playground! This pointy icicle could slice through a firm glass window! As it glistened in the sunlight it slowly, bit by bit, melted and left a glowing, shimmering puddle that lay underneath! The next morning the sun shone like never before, it left the other icicles' bodies swimming helplessly deep down below on the hot concrete ground! But not this icicle, he held strong and stayed gripping onto the wooden shed... until finally, he took one last breath, and fell brutally on the rock-hard ground!

Amy Dickson (11)
St Joseph's Catholic School, Malmesbury

The No-Named Dragon

There once lived a dragon who had no name, he sat in his cave all alone until one day, a brave little boy came to the cave and looked around. 'Hello,' he said curiously.
'Hello, come here,' said the dragon.
The boy came closer to the dragon, 'What is your name?' the boy asked.
'I don't have one!' said the dragon sadly.
'I'll help you find your name, don't worry!'
The boy sat beside the dragon, thinking and thinking and thinking! At last the boy leapt up from the cold cave floor, and said, 'I've got it, it's... Buruka!'

Mia Adams (11)
St Joseph's Catholic School, Malmesbury

I Hate Real Madrid

'Yay! I've just got chosen to be the captain for Real Madrid.' As Bob ran towards the stadium he saw tons of screaming fans. His first match went well, although he didn't do anything that night. 'Let's take a selfie,' shouted John.
'Oh wait, my mum is here now.'
The next match went so, so badly, he was changed from striker to ball boy. Bob was so upset and angry he went back home, ate some food and moved out. He never wanted to see Real Madrid ever again so he changed sports and moved to America to play baseball.

Nataniel Henryk Koszyk (11)
St Joseph's Catholic School, Malmesbury

A New Species Has Been Found!

Deer. Lovely little things they are, real dears, but they are a bit weird and I'm about to tell you why. I saw one yesterday and it looked a little odd. It had two legs instead of four; a walking stick; a bristly chin and grey hair. It was walking over the road mumbling, 'Ow! Ow!' with each step, most remarkable. Before, I was going around saying, 'Deer don't speak! They're always in such a rush to get away!' But I was wrong, besides I've only seen the brown ones with four legs. *New species*!

Jessica Turner (10)
St Joseph's Catholic School, Malmesbury

Untitled

'Soldiers, there have been sightings of the enemy, they are moving towards us, we need an arm-' *Bang*!
'What was that?' *Bang*! This time something happened, part of the wall broke and a tank drove in, it was followed by fifty soldiers. They were already shooting. Logan and Tom were the first to pick up their guns followed by the others. 'Logan, they're surrounding the tank, if we blow the tank up we will kill them,' Tom said over the roar of the guns. Logan sprinted to the gun rack and got an RPG and fired. He smiled smugly.

Alex Hopwood (11)
St Lawrence CE Primary School, Lechlade

The Unusual Truck Driver

One dark, foggy day at a very important game it was Man United vs West Ham, in the FA Cup Final. Thousands of people came to watch the game. Then suddenly out of nowhere everyone heard a car inside the stadium. A massive green truck drove onto the pitch. A load of skull faced men came sprinting onto the pitch. A boy called Joe jumped down from the seating area and onto the nice green grass to fight the evil skull people. The skull people fought Joe but Joe won in the end so the match could carry on.

Joe Albert George Griffiths (10)
St Lawrence CE Primary School, Lechlade

Wolfgang Amadeus Mozart First Tour - 1762

My father had taken my mother, sister and I on tour to play music for all the sovereigns. I had toured around many places. However, I was yet to play for the Emperor and Empress of Vienna. As we arrived at the entrance to the Imperial Court, I started to panic. What if I can't remember what to play, and make a complete fool of myself? The grand doors opened. The Emperor and Empress were right before my eyes. Thankfully, I played my best. When I finished, I sprung onto the Empress and kissed her on the cheek in relief!

Emilia Alice Matano (11)
St Lawrence CE Primary School, Lechlade

Alice In A Curious Forest

One summer's day there was a girl named Alice and she had a younger sister named Sasha, they both decided to go to the forest for the day. When they were about to go, Sasha said, 'Why don't we use time travel?'
'Great idea,' said Alice.
When they got there they stopped, looked at each other and started to think. 'Where are we?' said the two girls at the same time. So they went for a wander and then before they could say anything they both fainted. When they woke up they were back home and it was all a dream.

Alannah King (11)
St Lawrence CE Primary School, Lechlade

How I Killed Her Grandmother

I remember a little girl, walking down a nearby lane. I was hiding in the bushes and thought I would greet her. I saw that she had a picnic basket in her hand, and asked where she was going. 'Grandmother's,' was the reply. I was hungry for them both. So, I distracted her and ran for the grandmother's house. I devoured her. Suddenly, I heard the girl again, rushed into Grandmother's clothes, and pretended to be her. Unfortunately, a man came by and ruined the fun. I should never have done it, because now my belly is full of rocks!

Imogen Rebecca Hobbs
St Lawrence CE Primary School, Lechlade

Super Sparkie And Lightning Leo, The Crime Fighting Super Gerbils

It was a stormy night, I was running on my wheel, the lightning struck the wheel.

A few days later I discovered I had super powers so I sewed an outfit and cape, my superhero name was Super Sparkle. I dug through the sand dust to our house. Leo moaned, 'How come *you* get powers, it's not fair!' I told him he had to run on the wheel to get powers, but on a stormy night. He did! So we are superhero brothers, Lightning Leo and Super Sparkle, of course with matching outfits. Crime fighting brothers forever.

Rebecca Hooper (10)
St Lawrence CE Primary School, Lechlade

The Egg Stone

Scorch was a purple dragon who lived in a cave on the north side of Norway. Scorch's most prized possession was a large, speckled blue stone. He had found it rolling down a hill last Tuesday and adopted it. One day, the stone began to wobble and crack. Scorch looked at it in surprise. Suddenly, a tiny head popped out of the stone. Scorch was amazed, the stone wasn't a stone, it was an egg! The head was followed by a body and then a tail. Scorch picked up the baby dragon and cared for it like his own, forever.

Lauren Watkins (11)
St Lawrence CE Primary School, Lechlade

The Ghost's Return

It was midnight, James couldn't get to sleep, he felt as if somebody was in his room. Then a girl appeared, she was almost transparent, he finally found out that she was a ghost. He ran straight for the door, lamps were falling on the floor. James just didn't care. The door was locked and the key wasn't where it normally was. He was trapped. The ghost was coming, each step a louder thud, when she was about six centimetres away, James' hand started to glow and the ghost evaporated, he was gobsmacked. 'Amy you failed, James, I'm coming!'

Finnley Mark Thomas (10)
St White's School, Cinderford

Steve The Hero

Steve wasn't an ordinary owl. He was normal during the day, but what the citizens of Anamiltopia didn't realise was that there was two parts to Steve, one was normal, the next was unimaginable. Steve usually saved people but the phone call he received Tuesday morning was breathtaking. Time-Bomb the evil penguin had Steve's sister Amanda in his clutches! He traced the phone call and discovered his sister in a ticky-tocky mountain cave! Time-Bomb gripped Amanda's hand and said, 'Your time is running out and tick-tock, tick-tock!' Then he slowly walked away. Time-Bomb noticed Amanda's sigh of relief, it was Optimus-Owl

Jemma Harrison
St White's School, Cinderford

The War Of Races!

Today on Mars there was a war between predators and aliens. Predators were deadly soldiers fighting for their race. Meanwhile on Earth, Joseph, Max and Jack were making a teleporter and it was a success. What they didn't know was an alien came through without them knowing, until a scientist came in and shouted, 'Turn it off!' But they didn't, in fact they ran in and it took a century to get through to Mars but it actually took a second. When they got to Mars they saw an alien run up and try to kill Jack!

Cameron Nichol (10)
St White's School, Cinderford

Hammer Vs Hydra!

'You know the mission, let's go!' Hammer and his loyal partner Dick sped off. Their mission was to spy on Hydra. Hammer was a special spy, not just because he was stealthy, he was a hedgehog. When they arrived at Hydra's base, Hammer crawled through the window and disabled the alarms so Dick could come in. They took out the guards and crawled through the air vents until they were on top of a Hydra meeting. They found out all about Hydra's plan, then Dick fell through the roof! Running back to base, Hammer had a heart attack that killed him!

Thom Williams (10)
St White's School, Cinderford

The Day That Super Dog Saved The World

One day in a peaceful land or maybe a not so peaceful land Super Dog rested with his beloved family. His family treated him with respect. Then he heard a huge bang which was pretty scary. He went to see what was out there. A mysterious figure appeared out of the scary dark ship. He said to Super Dog, 'I must get all the games and puppies.'
'Well you won't get your hands on my puppies or Mr Game's games.'
'Well I can see his ship from here.'
'No, you won't get them.' Super Dog pushed him. He flew away.

Cody David Andrew Reynolds (10)
St White's School, Cinderford

Mission To A New Life

'I cannot believe I found that spider but I have to bring it to the lab,' spoke Max, but at that moment he heard rustling in the man-eating bushes. 'That's odd, nothing can hide in there or it would be eaten alive,' Max whispered to himself. Then he heard a blood-curdling hiss. Max turned around and standing behind him was a tall shadow-like creature. Max started running through the man-eating forest. One snagged him but before the creature could eat him another creature stopped it, it wanted lunch too.

Max Thomas (10)
St White's School, Cinderford

Planet Unicorn

'I'm finally on a new planet, it should be called Planet Unicorn,'
Sally announced. On the planet were unicorns with fairies on.
Instead of rain it was raining sweets. There were no problems ever!
'Hello, we are in charge. We will give you a room,' Polly unicorn
told her.
'Thank you for this beautiful room you've given me,' Sally told them
cheerfully.
'If you are hungry or thirsty you can eat your bedroom, if you want
to,' Polly told her.
After, she was sleeping. When she woke up, a chocolate lake
appeared. 'Yum! I'll eat it,' Sally shouted loudly.

Maisie Bullock (10)
St White's School, Cinderford

The Two Children Time Travelling

In the docks, Callum and Huey were sitting down, all of a
sudden a portal appeared from thin air. Callum walked into it and
disappeared and Huey followed him. They realised that they were
time travelling to Dinosaur World. When they got there they saw
a T-rex and it looked angry. Then, before they knew it, they were
running for their life. They ran all around the strange place, then
they quickly ran to the portal and travelled back to their time. Then
they ran back home and told their mums and they didn't believe
them.

Callum Phillips (10)
St White's School, Cinderford

A Day In The Life Of A Scout

'I think it's just you and me now,' Joe said to me. We were running through the wilderness trying to find shelter after time travelling to a ghost land. Joe and I were brave warriors trying to find other time travellers in every different dimension. Sometimes it's dangerous but mostly we can cope. Here's how we did it. I was in the woods with my Scout group and I was behind Joe (my leader) until he stumbled across a little gauntlet lying on the ground. We both picked it up and *zap*! We found ourselves in a different dimension, lost.

Jack Robinson (10)
St White's School, Cinderford

Underwater World

Underwater lived a dolphin who had two friends. The two friends were a clownfish and a seal. They lived in the middle of the Pacific Ocean, where a vast boat sank in the middle of the ocean. The seal, that was called Sammy, showed Dave and Canter all of her tricks. Dave did a backflip out of the water and landed on Canter. Canter swam up from under Dave and then Dave stroked Canter with his tail. They had a party under the blue sea and then Dave and Sammy pulled sixty party poppers, then they all swam away.

Aimee Wilson (10)
St White's School, Cinderford

The Adventures Of Supercat

There was a baby kitten that lived on his own and grew up to be Supercat. He fought crime and saved people from the evil Dr Bionic. Dr Bionic was a villain that wanted to take over the world, but with Supercat in the way he couldn't.
One day, Dr Bionic decided to burn the school down but Supercat went to the rescue. He swooped down to the school, got a hose and put the fire out. He kicked the door down and got everyone out. Then he caught Dr Bionic and put him in jail. He was awarded a medal.

Sophie Whitfield (10)
St White's School, Cinderford

Super Cat Saves A Dog

In an alley in the big city lived a cat. Not an ordinary cat, a super cat. In his alley was a secret door, inside was Super Cat's hideout. He had super hearing so he could hear any call of distress. Speaking of that, a call of distress, it was a bark, it must be Jazz the dog. Let's take a look through the periscope, there he is in the green fluorescent light, he's being abducted by aliens. *Whoosh*! Super Cat dashed to the rescue. *Pow*! *Bang*! *Crash*! He karate kicked the alien, saved Jazz and off he flew. Hooray!

Liam Bodley (10)
St White's School, Cinderford

Batty To The Rescue

One day in Hollywood it wouldn't stop raining. Mrs Gracey went for a walk with her greyhound, then suddenly, evil Doctor Porkchop grabbed her and took her to his secret lab. Batman sprung into action. As quick as a flash he was in Porky's lab, he jumped to the fourth floor. 'One more floor and then I will save Mrs Gracey,' whispered Batman, 'one, two, three, jump...' but before he could jump he saw robots coming up the stairs, he attacked and won! 'Come on Porky, bring it on.' *Bang*! *Crash*! *Boom*! Batman grabbed Mrs Gracey. She's saved!

Anwen Fay Osborn (10)
St White's School, Cinderford

Lifting The Titanic Out Of The Ocean

Somewhere in the middle of the Atlantic a mermaid, lionfish, shark and whale were looking to find all the pieces of the famous ship, Titanic. It took them at least two weeks to find all of it, but they had to go to the local shop to get the super strong ship glue. They must have bought ten gallons of glue. They pieced the Titanic together but they had to replace most of the rivets. It took forever. But finally it was ready to set sail, they lifted it out of the blue sapphire, glistening, radiant ocean.

Charlotte Tuck (10)
St White's School, Cinderford

Super Girl Saves The Day!

Once there was a girl hanging from the roof top. She was screaming for help. Then out of nowhere came a girl, not any ordinary girl, no it was Super Girl. She swooped down and grabbed the little girl and took her back to safety and then she said, 'Thank you.'
Super Girl said, 'No please, it's what I do.' Then she heard a voice, it was evil Meat Boy, Super Girl got caught. Then came Miss Pie Face and unlocked her, then Super Girl got back to her job, after all superheroes never give up. Hooray!

Megan Trigg (10)
St White's School, Cinderford

The Murderous Mystery

Long ago in a land called Anitopia, there was a murderous mystery on 50B Hedgro Lane. A hedgehog, Paul 27, was murdered. Simon the detective owl was on the case. First, he met friends and foes to ask questions about this mystery. No help. Next was the house. Then, in a far off room, there was the smell of rotting blood. Was it him? Yes, but why was he holding a knife? Another mystery. Simon looked at the finger prints. But how? It can't be! He checked. He had found a video. Simon watched. The murder was him, Paul (hedgehog).

Rosie Jones (9)
St White's School, Cinderford

Fight Of The Kings

One sunny day King Charles was sailing to France to have a fight with The Joker. He was taking his well trained son with him. Just after he docked, he left his son at the port. They got ready for the fight. After three days of fighting The Joker was dead. The king and his son had survived, so they changed their sail to sail home.

Aiden Toms (8)
Sopley Primary School, Christchurch

Captain Pickles Vs Finn

Finn was trying to find his diamond magic wand so he set off on an adventure. A giant helped him on his way until he found Mr Pickles' house. He opened the door and heard a voice, 'Here for your glittering magical wand?'
'Give it back.'
'If you battle me?'
The gods were watching, they gave him a gold sword and armour. Finn was in trouble but his sword was strong enough. He bashed it into Captain Pickles, killed him and claimed his magic wand. He wanted to put his wand next to his enchanted sword but it was gone.

Denas Bitinas (9)
Sopley Primary School, Christchurch

The Adventure

The rich king opened the letter with a heart beating harder than a jack-hammer! It was from Vitruvius, he was scared. It said, 'I will kill your two sons, Harry and Jack, you have eighty days.'
'Oh no,' said the king, 'there is a big battle ahead.' He couldn't sleep, all he could think about was his two sons fighting the most powerful man in the world. Vitruvius had a weakness, it was diamonds. They added diamonds to their weapons so they would win. Vitruvius was dead. They sailed back and everybody was fine.

Sydney Walthall (7)
Sopley Primary School, Christchurch

The Princess And The Chihuahua

Because of her beauty, Princess Gabriella was hated by the jealous wicked witch, whose black soul had turned her ugly. One day Gabriella was in the meadow picking flowers, when a voice said, 'Come and get free Chihuahuas.' She bought one. Meanwhile the witch made a spell to poison her. *Bang!* Lightning struck 'Now,' said the witch, 'she will be mine!' Suddenly it was pitch-black. Gabriella cuddled her Chihuahua. An old lady offered her some lemonade. They both drank but the witch got the glasses mixed up and fell down dead. Gabriella lived happily with her Chihuahuas.

Libby Mae Hines (8)
Sopley Primary School, Christchurch

The Fight Over Chocolate

At that moment, Mia's feet began to shrink. Her voice squeaked and she ended up no bigger than an ant! The same happened to Annie, Josh and Jake until they were scurrying around the table legs. None of them knew it was magic chocolate. None of them knew except for the shopkeeper. 'What are we going to do?' they cried. 'We need to help each other.' Then they said sorry to each other for fighting over the chocolate. To solve the problem, they ate some more chocolate and grew back to normal size again. What a journey!

Danielle Wynn (9)
Sopley Primary School, Christchurch

Target Attack

It was a snowy Christmas in Scampy Village and the villagers were very excited. What they didn't know was that Lee Bear (the best cake maker in the village) was trapped in the prison cage because the evil Hit The Target had caught him and was forcing him to make cakes. Scampy saw Hit The Target leave the prison and wondered why? He took his bow and arrow to rescue the trapped Lee Bear. Hit The Target was really angry and shouted he would come back. So Scampy and Lee had there Christmas lunch and were really happy he was gone.

Milly Laidlaw (9)
Sopley Primary School, Christchurch

Zombie Terror

Zombie armies came and attacked the village of Horrible Vile. Fifteen were captured. 'We're going to rescue them!' shouted Henry.

'Brains,' moaned a zombie. Henry slayed him and entered the castle. Inside they killed millions of zombies but the zombie king escaped through a portal. Henry followed him to a place called End. The king drank a black potion turning into a gigantic purple dragon. Henry realised that he needed to destroy the crystals in the tower. Weaker now, the dragon could no longer fly. Henry attacked him with a sword, he exploded and the villagers were free.

Henry Richardson (8)
Sopley Primary School, Christchurch

Ghost Busters!

I was fast asleep in my cosy bed when suddenly something breezy like a ghost pushed me onto the hard floor. What was it and why am I on the floor? It wasn't my dad because his breath smelt like last night's curry and it wasn't my dog's breath because his breath smelt like fish so it must be something bad. I was terrified, I ran down the stairs and called Ghostbusters who came as quick as possible... When they arrived they got the ghost by shooting it.

Dylan Patten (9)
Sopley Primary School, Christchurch

The Village

Mia and Lily-Ann were in the village dancing and entertaining people. Jack and Joshua put a spell on them so they talked in a poem kind of way. Mia found an amazing spell in their spell book. 'Abracadabra spit ploo! Yes, I did it, now I can speak properly.' The boys started being nice, but had they changed? Yes of course they had.
Mia said to Jack, 'I have nowhere to sleep tonight because there's an ants' nest.'
'You can sleep in my bed tonight with my cat.' They finally got married and lived happily ever after.

Gabriella Southon (8)
Sopley Primary School, Christchurch

The Bed And The Cat

As I crawled behind the sofa the grumpy giant was snoozing upstairs. My mission was to get to the bed. You go through the big sofa, climb up the steps, wiggle past the door, scram up the blanket and finally you're in the bed but that's all a dream. Here goes, I'm travelling through the sofa, I'm out, let's jump upstairs, it's difficult. I'm at the top. I remember the big door. I sneak past, it stinks. I finally make it, let's go and climb up the blanket. I leap up and fall into the bed. It's like a cloud.

Jena Rea Wallis (8)
Sopley Primary School, Christchurch

Good Bones Vs Broken Bones

In the sky flies a blue village with blue trees and blue houses. It is an enchanted place. Good Bones was gardening in the village, he carefully dug up a magic book that let him fly and sparks flew from his bony hands. Meanwhile Broken Bones had seen the magic book and wanted to steal the magic book so he could take control of the village. When nobody was looking Broken Bones quickly stole the magic book and was frightening lots and lots of people. But Good Bones wasn't scared, he flashed and burnt Broken Bones up.

Justin Ivett (8)
Sopley Primary School, Christchurch

Time Travel Adventure!

I went through the doorway. My future self was saying, 'How can I serve you?' Eloise was my friend; if she was Queen, then why was I her servant? I decided to ask the future me for help, she sent me through the ancient door. I found the teenage me with Eloise, she was showing me her Peronol doll, leaving she forgot her backpack. That night a burglar stole Peronol.
In the morning Eloise accused me, I was distraught. I knew the truth, I stepped back through the door. We approached the Queen. Surprisingly she believed me! I was saved.

Daisy Tuddenham (8)
Sopley Primary School, Christchurch

The Faraway Tree: The Land Of Time Travel

'What's wrong Moon-Face?' cried Eloise.
'If we don't stop the Time War the faraway tree will be destroyed,' he cried.
'The bad Time-Lord Rassilon has killed the king, Queen Daisy wants revenge.'
All of a sudden an owl came out of the darkness. 'I'm Queen Daisy's pet, come and hide in her palace for the Time War.' So they went to the palace, all of a sudden the door burst open.
'Doctor!' cried Queen Daisy.
'Please kill Rassilon,' they pleaded. They watched the fight in terror. A blood-curdling scream was heard. Rassilon had died. The doctor had won. Hurray!

Eloise Samantha Elizabeth Wall (8)
Sopley Primary School, Christchurch

Bob And Dust

'What was that noise?'
'I have no idea!' said Dust.
'You go first,' said Bob
'OK,' said Dust, 'look, I see a massive shadow far away.'
'Well what do you do when you see a big fat monster? Kill it.'
Yes, Dust and Bob were going to kill the big giant in the cave. 'Get your sword ready,' said Bob. They were going to the giant and he had a little man in his hand. 'Oh no!' shouted Bob. They had to save the man, 'Don't worry little man, hold right on!'
Bash! The giant was dead.

Jack Dennis (8)
Sopley Primary School, Christchurch

Rocky Balboa

Suddenly in the deep, dark forest, there was a noise, Rocky kept on walking and he saw Ivan Drago, he attacked him before their boxing match. Rocky beat him, he had to go to hospital. Rocky got home, he started training.
A few days later the fight came on, his wife was really scared, Rocky wasn't scared, he just wanted to fight. He'd only lost one fight, he was really good at boxing. His muscle weighed about two hundred pounds. Ivan Drago cheated because he used steroids, Rocky didn't cheat, he did really good because he trained really well. He won!

Stanley Doe (8)
Sopley Primary School, Christchurch

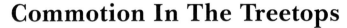

Commotion In The Treetops

'Fire! Fire! Bushfire!' I shouted. Frantically, my monkey family grabbed our things and set off. The jungle rang with shouts and screams. We swung away through the trees. I slipped! Down I fell into the white witch's net and she carried me away to be her slave. 'Help!' I screamed. The palace reeked of something disgusting. I had to be a maid and do all the dirtiest jobs. It was devastating. Suddenly there was a rumble and the palace split apart. An earthquake had freed me. I grabbed a vine and swung home.

Harriet Melling (8)
Sopley Primary School, Christchurch

City Showdown

Four unknown boys crept into a dark gloomy cave. Before their eyes were four mysterious dragon eggs. In front of them were weapons and suits which they put on.
On the news they heard that three villains were trying to destroy New York. They knew they must act. As they were going their dragon eggs hatched. 'Woohoo!' they all shouted as they flew off to New York on their new dragons.
'Argh!' There was a scream from a school. The boys fought their way through just in time. Capturing all the bad guys and putting them in prison.

Brodie Dylan Yates (8)
Sopley Primary School, Christchurch

Commotion In The Ocean

Neela listened. Strangely the sea was rough. Suddenly walls
started crumbling... She hurried to her friend Corsa. Together they
shot down the corridor. The once sparkling hall was destroyed. A
merman rode a scaly dragon, blood drooling from its poisonous
fangs; eyes burning hot and flashing in rage. 'Catch them!' he
roared. Black arrows shot through the water towards them.
Captured, the girls were handcuffed, netting wrapped devilishly
tight around them. At Draco's camp they were questioned. They
lied! Shaking, Neela cast her mermaid magic to unpick the cuffs.
They swam out sneakily until... 'Stop right there!' boomed a voice!

Amy Wood (9)
Sopley Primary School, Christchurch

Wowing Witches And Brilliant Blobby

'Argh!' screamed Amy and Abi startled.
'What? Where? Who?' As the Earth shook, terror reigned down on
Earth as Blobby landed... 'It's Blobby!' they said nervously.
Abi and Amy were extremely powerful witches. They danced
around the bubbling cauldron casting spells to make Blobby shrink.
'I adore our wands,' said Amy. Made of wood and as beautiful
as nature, they twisted up with daisies. Now they had to hunt for
Blobby, they found him in a forest, they shrunk him and fixed all the
damage. Now Blobby is a little pet so cute. Will the shrinking spell
wear off?

Molly May Burdock (9)
Sopley Primary School, Christchurch

Mega-P Vs Streak

One day in Bournemouth, David Streak sat in his home. The Streaks and the Patels were enemies. Peter Patel had enough; he became a Cyborg, he was Mega-P. He went to the Streaks' house and killed everyone except David, because he was out. When David got home he vowed to kill Mega-P. David found the Patel lair, where he found a killer raptor but killed it. He found Mega-P ready to kill.
They fought for days and days, eventually David Streak won. He then got a life, family and a pet and lived happily ever after.

Tomas Lopez-Johnson (10)
Sopley Primary School, Christchurch

The Curse Of The Evil King

Princess Isabel was bored. Her pet fairy, Gabriella gave her a delicious snack. There was none left for King Aiden, so he went to the royal shop. When he got there he was shocked, a witch's hut stood in its place. Furious, he went inside to see a hunchback witch. Maybe she might make a delicious snack spell. She tricked him; the potion turned him into a shaggy monster. Taking the monster to the palace, she smashed up the kitchen. Gabriella made a potion to heal King Aiden. She splashed it on him and he turned into himself again.

Francesca Blythe (8)
Sopley Primary School, Christchurch

Untitled

Once upon a time in the deepest, darkest part of the forest, there lived a jolly, intelligent also courageous dwarf. This dwarf was no typical dwarf, he had awesome magical powers. Underneath the tallest tree, over the wobbly green bridge, across the worn shabby stepping stones leads you to the dwarf's secret hideout! However, one of the dwarfs was horrifyingly spiteful and he wanted to steal the jolly dwarf's precious spell book. His aim was to kidnap the jolly dwarf's by using a net trap, but the trap backfired trapping the vicious dwarf in his own gloomy trap...

Shirley Pearce (10)
The Springfields Academy, Calne

Untitled

In a mystical, spooky, hidden wood, in the middle of a strange, unlikely valley; the sunlit glow of an old stable door leads the way to an underground, secluded sanctuary. A cluster of ugly, petite, vile dwarfs who are only a foot high, are interestingly clothed in moss green jackets, also wooden clogs that are yellow like the glow of the sun. Surprisingly, the illusive dwarfs have a dilemma! Humans are intrusive beings who will spoil the dwarfs' precious secrets. The dwarfs purposefully deceive the intrusive humans by leaving riches to lure them in to an opaque hole of doom!

Harrison Wild (11)
The Springfields Academy, Calne

85

The Hunt

As I turn the corner he sees me, then he eyes me up as his next victim with joy in his eyes. I start running for my life. I know he will catch me up. But I see him turn the corner. He spots another victim, phew, I start to relax. I hide behind a tree and then I cautiously look around. Suddenly he leaps on me and narrowly misses my chest. He then swings out and gets me, damn! I'm 'it' and then the bell stops our game. 'You are 'it' next break,' they all say.

James Allen (11)
Tockington Manor School, Bristol

Black Out

One horrible day, a boy called Justin was in grief, because his dog Fred, was ill. He was determined to find a cure for his disease. All of a sudden, everything turned black and Justin found himself on a ship with a map. He was curious as to where the cross was, so he set sail and before he knew it he was at the location. On a hot plain desert island. So he started digging. Suddenly he hit a chest. There in the box was a cure. Then he woke up in hospital with his dog at his side.

Angus Duncan (11)
Tockington Manor School, Bristol

Aztec Gold

I was running, the golden sculpture was in my hands. The Aztecs were chasing me from their temple. They were catching up with me, their hands reaching out to pull me back. My ship came into sight. 'Come on,' I heard one person saying, 'quickly they're catching up.'
The man said, 'Only a few paces left.'
Another man said, 'I was so close to the ship, I could picture us beating the Aztecs,' when, 'tag, now you have to return the flag to our base!'

Jonathan Baguley (10)
Tockington Manor School, Bristol

A Day At The Zoo

Every day Rachel visited an ordinary zoo in an ordinary town. People wondered why she never got bored. She always ate the same food at the same time with the same friends, saw the same animals and took the same route. She did this every day no matter what the weather was, be it rain, snow, hail or heat-wave. People started to think there was something fishy about her behaviour. She smelt like fish, she loved fish and she even liked to swim with them. People even called her Flippy. Rachel was in fact a penguin!

Talia Curtis (11)
Tockington Manor School, Bristol

The Great Runaway

I'm out; this is the most exhilarating escape yet, not stuck behind bars anymore! I run into a dark, damp, dingy alley. I shall live here until I am found. I'm going day to day eating scraps out of bins; and then I see him, the man! He's here to take me away, I can't be stuck behind bars; not anymore, I run but they have vehicles. I'm on my bare feet. After a mile they finally catch me, my feet are vigorously pounding with pain. I am taken in the biggest vehicle of all back to my lion enclosure.

Maddie Ella Appleton Summers (11)
Tockington Manor School, Bristol

The Great Escape

This is my chance to escape. The gate is open and finally I can run off to my long-lost cousins in South America. This is it. I'm out, through the gate and out of the drive. I'm so lucky to have such long and speedy legs, he will never catch me now. No. The car, I forgot about the car. I can hear that dreaded engine. I'm going as fast as I can, but the car is faster. It is coming closer. It has cornered me. He's out. 'Come on Bart, you silly alpaca, let's get you back home.'

Tabitha Huby (11)
Tockington Manor School, Bristol

The End

Walking up those stairs, towards my fate knowing every second this was the end, even though it hadn't even begun. Breathing heavily I sat down staring at the emptiness of the room. So silent, I could hear my heart beating, so cold I could see my breath in the air. Suddenly, I heard the sound of cruel footsteps coming towards me, and then I saw it, the object that was to determine my life's story. She placed it on my lap. I opened my mouth to scream, but no sound came out. Then the figure spoke, 'Your exam starts now!'

Georgina Isobel Loring (11)
Tockington Manor School, Bristol

The Story We All Know...

The prince heard the sweet singing once again, as he rode through the evergreen forest to his love. He stopped outside the towering prison. The prince yelled out at the top of his voice, 'Rapunzel, let down your hair!' Immediately blonde hair came tumbling down the enormous tower. Gripping tightly to the hair he struggled to climb up the tower. Finally he reached the top. Inside it was dark and there wasn't a spot of light.
'I'm here,' she said. The prince walked over then screamed as two golden fangs were revealed, 'Time to say goodbye!' Rapunzel said grinning.

Anya Constantinescu (11)
Tockington Manor School, Bristol

Tench!

'Please matron, not the 'Tench' please.' I was trapped, this place made me feel as if I was no one and the 'Tench', was the worst punishment of them all. The Tench was a dark, gloomy place with rats. It was so dark you didn't know how long you had been in there for, but I had to remember that I was Hetty Feather foundling number 25629. My mother had abandoned me here when I was a baby, and this was my life. There was a knock on the library door. I needed to take James home. We could visit tomorrow!

Rachel Shutt (11)
Tockington Manor School, Bristol

The Hand

The murder of Hunter John, two years ago is a mystery. The hunter had nobody round his house because nobody knew him until the day the beekeeper came round. The hunter showed the beekeeper his collection, then he showed him a hand chained against the wall strong enough to hold an elephant. That is why he kept guns.
The next day the beekeeper came over and found the hunter dead with a finger in his mouth and a hand mark around his neck. Furthermore, the victim had a wooden fake hand so the strong hand was his.

William Sheppard (11)
Tockington Manor School, Bristol

The Adventure Of The Easter Bunny

Once upon a time, keeping himself occupied, the Easter bunny was cleaning his golden banana sweet that was in his chocolate chip house.

Later that day, Menacing Monkey and his team came to steal the sweet. The Easter bunny got his big feet ready. *Pow!* The Easter bunny defeated them. One of the monkeys survived but he came out with the fake banana sweet which the Easter bunny had swapped. As Menacing Monkey got up the Easter bunny said, 'I'm sorry, I just don't want anyone to get my banana sweet.' The Easter bunny and Menacing Monkey became friends.

Courtney Toomer-Hall
Turlin Moor Community School, Poole

Splat

Once upon a time, there lived a giraffe but this was no ordinary giraffe! Setting off on her daily routine, she knew today was the day! Bringing happiness to people was her passion.

Heading to work, she was convinced that everyone wanted to be as happy as her. Therefore, her mission was to turn everyone into a giraffe! So far only one man hadn't been turned. Spotting her, the man ran his fastest so he wouldn't get splattered into a giraffe, managing to catch her with a net and putting her in a zoo. No more splattering for her!

Angel Hansford
Turlin Moor Community School, Poole

The Five Armies

The battle started between the five armies. They were all fighting over the great castle. Swords clashed, arrows were flying and bodies died. Just then, the army in the castle spotted the greatest army approaching.
Their captain was an enormous monster called Zinyang. Suddenly, Robbie (the captain of the people that lived in the castle) remembered the last war where he chopped his arm off; something he didn't want repeated. All of a sudden, a bomb shook the castle then it began to tumble. Robbie and Zinyang stood in the middle of the wreckage as the great castle fell...

Tristan Reece Flanagan (11)
Turlin Moor Community School, Poole

Cockroach Invasion

Once upon a time there lived a doughnut called Bob. He wasn't any ordinary doughnut - he had a sugar glaze with a custard filling. He could fly, shoot custard and had unbeatable strength.
Bob went to bed in his box. He heard something. So he woke up and got up just in time to see the back of some mysterious creatures. He walked round the corner of his box and saw... cockroaches! He thought to himself, *I'm being invaded!* So he quickly went to battle them but changed his mind and became friends with them all.

Kieran John George (11)
Turlin Moor Community School, Poole

The Menacing Monkey And Fruit

Once upon a time, there lived a menacing monkey who hated humans eating his five a day. He believed that all fruit should only be eaten by monkeys. Being the menacing monkey that he was, his usual task was to swing down from his tree and swipe picnics for himself and his monkey friends. However, one day, his task went horribly wrong and he was caught by a waiting human. As his punishment he never ate a piece of fruit ever again.

Lilyaleah Musselwhite
Turlin Moor Community School, Poole

The Mystery Fish

Trying to solve the mystery of the mystery fish! The small girl adventurer was underwater trying to find it but she kept bumping into all sorts of underwater sea creatures. The sea creatures were fish, sharks, starfish and jellyfish. But finally she found the mystery fish. Then unfortunately the jellyfish stung her! At that very moment she died. After a while the girl's adventurer's mum hadn't seen her for a while so she went to find her. She finally found her at the bottom of the sea, she tried to save her until she realised she had to give up.

Madison Deller (8)
Westrop Primary School, Swindon

The Cheese Touch

From space fell a mouldy cheese, it fell into the same ocean as SpongeBob. Guess what, when SpongeBob found it he adored it. He was going to sell it at the Krusty Crab but it meant too much to him.

One morning SpongeBob had it for breakfast, his eyes swirled, he must have the cheese touch! Whenever SpongeBob saw anyone he chased them everywhere to lose it. Unfortunately SpongeBob couldn't get anyone.

One week later, he finally passed it onto Mr Crabs. 'That felt weird,' whispered SpongeBob, 'I need to get home!'

He fell asleep for three whole weeks.

Ben David Stratford (9)
Westrop Primary School, Swindon

One Evil Turtle

One dramatic day an evil turtle called Terry was trying to take over the world, he was trying to take over the world because his enemy was Nemo and he was the king of the world. Nemo saw him and gave him some magic beans and the evil Terry fell into a pot of lava, he burned to death and died. The world was saved from the villain Terry. They had a celebration.

Leah Holly Wood (9)
Westrop Primary School, Swindon

The Underwater Mystery

It all started when there lived two fish called Nemo and Dory. Three days later, Nemo drank a potion and turned evil. Nemo tried to kill Dory but Dory was too interested in her shadow, and kept saying, 'Katie, get out of my way I can't see.'
But several months later, Nemo got behind Dory's fin and *bang! Crash!* Dory was dead.
'Cut! Only twelve scenes to go,' shouted the director. The underwater world was safe, then Nemo wasn't evil anymore. Everyone was happy that Nemo wasn't evil. Especially Nemo and Dory. Nemo and Dory were finally happy.

Molly Louise Carter (9)
Westrop Primary School, Swindon

The Cliff Of Terror

It all started in a dark and scary forest where the cliff lived. There was a prince called George, he heard a sound then he just realised that it was Princess Georgina. George ran as quick as he could then he fell off a cliff, luckily he landed on the castle. He broke into the castle and saved Princess Georgina. Then they fell in love and got married. Prince George killed King Tigger in a big fight, after then Prince George fell off the cliff. Georgina tried to save him.

Samantha Lewis (9)
Westrop Primary School, Swindon

The Beautiful Palace

Underwater in a palace there was a sparkling mermaid, she was called Sally. She went for a swim when suddenly she was trapped in a clam shell. She called for help. Just then all the mermaids came, then Sally was saved but then a storm came, the mermaids swam back to their palace as quickly as possible. The mermaids were safe and sound. The storm got louder and louder. But then it stopped, it was peaceful. After the storm was gone all the creatures came out and all the mermaids came out.

Daniel James Taylor (9)
Westrop Primary School, Swindon

The House Of Horror

It all started when a certain family moved into a creepy old house. It was 1946 when it all started. It was sold by Samuel Miles. The boy had the smallest room as his bedroom. When he walked in it the door shut, he thought it was his mum but it was not. Jack then went to bed. In his dream he was all alone in the school because everyone was dead thanks to the school cook. Suddenly the cook arrived to kill him. She found him and chopped him, until he died.

Matthew Widdop (8)
Westrop Primary School, Swindon

The Mixed-Up Missions

It all started with six humans called Melissa, Polly, Tasha, Dani and Maddie. Melissa is their mum and works at a secret agent club and she does really cool missions. That night she got a mission to find out who stole the famous statue.

The next day she saw a man taking the statue and he was wearing a black top and big boots with blue trousers. When she found out that he was just cleaning it she turned into an octopus and got trapped in a tank but she got eaten by a zombie at a restaurant.

Lucy Osborne (9)
Westrop Primary School, Swindon

The Sheep Man

It all started with a man called Dan, he owned a farm.

The next day he was working to win the biggest sheep award.

The next morning he was stabbed in the back. The man who stabbed him was his best friend!

The next day he was turned into a sheep then pushed off a cliff. Nobody knows why?

Harry Medlock (9)
Westrop Primary School, Swindon

George And The Giant Jelly

It all started a long time ago in an old wooden shack. A boy called George was in his dark, dusty kitchen. He saw a tasty jelly on the side of the table! It looked so delicious, he licked it to taste it. But it grew bigger! It made him bigger! So he got on the jelly. George saw lots of animals on the jelly, a pig, cow, donkey and a horse. One thing that was gross was the animals had no pupils. They looked starving. George made friends with them and had fun until they had eaten the jelly.

James Henderson (8)
Westrop Primary School, Swindon

The Accident

Ever since the incident Jeffery is close to death as he's about to fall. A superhero comes but... he sinks in the sand and he's never seen again. Surely something can save him to escape his death. The second superhero comes to save the day so he uses his jet-pack but drops his firework match in the sand. Suddenly it is on fire and the superhero saves him and flies into the sunset but instead he flies into a bird and falls and they die and they totally lived happily ever after I think.

Nayeeb Miah (8)
Westrop Primary School, Swindon

Whirlpool

As the waves splashed on the rock, people were in the sea having a great time. Now and then there were people disappearing under the sea. Susan was petrified although Susan still went in the sea with her friend Kirsty. They both jumped into the water and had fun. Suddenly Susan was trapped! She couldn't swim any more. Then, in a flash, she went but Kirsty saved her. All of a sudden Kirsty was sucked in and Susan shouted, 'Kirsty! Kirsty!' But nobody replied. She looked under the water but nobody was there so she cried and cried then died.

Jack Freddie Carter (9)
Westrop Primary School, Swindon

The Twist In Time

Suddenly the coach engine started to hiss, the coach moved. In a few hours Southrop school was at Blackpool Pier. The teacher, Mrs Mavis shouted, 'Everyone out in an orderly fashion and explore the pier.' Tash and Hetty ran out and immediately ran to the end of the pier.
'Hey what's that Tash?' Suddenly Hetty did a forward roll and they found her hanging off the pier!
'Hetty!' screamed Tash. Hetty heard a voice.
It was the Time Turner and he said, 'It doesn't have to be you.'
So Hetty said, 'Okay.' So Tash was hanging off the pier, she died!

Poppy Howarth-Barnes (9)
Westrop Primary School, Swindon

A Boring Old Lesson!

It was another old lesson on another boring day. It was literacy, in Miss Taylor's classroom, they were studying life cycles of different plants and animals. Then it all turned silent and miserable. It was pitch-black and all Ruby and Bethan could see was the faint outline of Finley and Tayler. Then disco lights started at the same time as a siren came to life. Suddenly... everyone started to moan weirdly then they all fainted. When they awoke they could not stop dancing wildly.

Bethan Grant (9)
Westrop Primary School, Swindon

Clown Escape

It all started when there was a family who moved into a haunted house and it was ninety years old. Fifty people had been killed in it. However, the next day, a little boy called John went to school but he couldn't drive so he had to walk one mile. He noticed something on the way, his street was really quiet but it was normally loud. Finally he got to school but it was really quiet. Then he saw a clown so he jumped in a bin and rolled off a cliff, *smack!* he has gone forever now.

George Phillip Webster (9)
Westrop Primary School, Swindon

The Little Sweetie Girl

A little girl was selling sweets on a snowy bitter evening. The little girl had bare feet and just a maiden dress on. That very evening she hadn't sold any sweets at all, her mother Anne was going to be furious. The little sweetie girl sat down on the freezing cold ground, she pulled out a sweet from her bag and held it tightly in her hand and imagined she was in a kind family. The little girl stood up and stumbled home, on the way she found a pound coin, she was pleased and skipped home, her parents weren't furious.

Ruby Gill (9)
Westrop Primary School, Swindon

The Maoam Stripe Dinosaur And Jeff

In France there was a mysterious creature which was a Maoam stripe dinosaur, who always ate Maoam stripes. In Jeff's house he had lots of giant Maoam stripes. Back out a few miles the prehistoric dinosaur could sense the lovely Maoam stripes. All of a sudden the dinosaur came charging down the street to Jeff's house. Suddenly, the dinosaur knocked down the building with his sharp spiked tail. Luckily Jeff survived, so did the Maoams. The fight commenced for the Maoam stripes. Suddenly the Maoam stripe dinosaur spiked Jeff with his super spiked tail. The dinosaur won the Maoam stripes!

Josh Hutchison (9)
Westrop Primary School, Swindon

Military Base (James Bond 007)

There was ten minutes left on the nuclear bomb. 'Sorry to scare you, my name is James Bond Aka 007. I was in a military base trying to find Commander Gold Eye. All of a sudden Gold Eye jumped out for a surprise attack then I threw Gold Eye into some lava.'

Samuel James Barber (8)
Westrop Primary School, Swindon

The Enchantment

As a girl called Ariadni was slowly walking through a dark and cold enchanted forest, Ariadni looked up at the sky and suddenly something flew over her head. Ariadni had been told when she was a child that once people had entered the enchanted forest they always thought that it was an evil witch called Sapphire causing all the enchantment. As she was thinking about that moment Sapphire's evil ghost Casper pushed over a wobbly gigantic tree so Ariadni ran and ran...

Sophie Dillingham (9)
Westrop Primary School, Swindon

The Haunted City

He was slowly swimming in the lake whilst the water slowly started to turn red, he'd started to sink. He saw an underwater haunted city! He found loads of ghosts and zombies, there was even a zombie king, also a massive gloop of slime. The boy investigated the haunted city and something chased him, he quickly started to swim back up but he got shot by a ghastly man. 'Argh!'

Jamal Barry (8)
Westrop Primary School, Swindon

Hairdresser Horror

Behind the door you could hear children muttering to their parents and a mum with a boy who hesitated to go in...
Suddenly, he found his courage and stumbled into the dark gloomy room one step at a time. Then his mother disappeared suspiciously, but he did not notice because he was too busy staring in anticipation at the gruesome heads and bodies on the jagged floor, also the windows were smashed and glass shattered everywhere!
Without warning he saw the hairdresser turn... 'Help!' he gulped loudly, he felt lost and sadly it was his turn. The curtain was twitching.

Isabelle Barratt (9)
Westrop Primary School, Swindon

Harry Sucks At Quidditch

Whoosh! Harry zoomed past the bulldozer dodging to the left. In the corner of his eyes, the snitch! Harry raced towards the snitch, however he saw Cedric flying towards him. Cedric was gaining on him five metres, three, two, one metre. Then Cedric caught up with Harry, the race was on. Harry was going to the snitch, his hand was a hair's length away but Cedric's hand was as well. Suddenly Harry saw a Dementor, it started to lift its hood, it was going to suck his soul. 'Cut!' shouted the director. Right now, Harry suddenly falls off his broomstick.

Jonjoe Rosato (8)
Westrop Primary School, Swindon

Haunted Hallways

Grace woke up. Suddenly she heard a noise, then Grace crept with fear to the door and saw an imprint of a ghost! Then she heard a deafening scream, Grace was horrified so she slammed the door and ran back to her bed with fear, she pulled the covers up quickly. Grace then screamed, 'Mum and Dad!' They ran to Grace then cuddled her so she fell asleep.

Hannah Wardroper (9)
Westrop Primary School, Swindon

Ghostly Green Hands

On a cursed beach there were two children named Amber and George. Amber had discovered a graveyard. She saw a grave that had the names: Amber and George. Suddenly, glowing green hands started to pop up everywhere. Amber and George's hearts were pumping out of their chests. Then a glowing green hand caught Amber and George by the ankle and whilst George's back was turned for five seconds, Amber was gone! Was there a curse from their grave that made them disappear? Or was it a quicksand pit? No one will ever know...

Jasmin Wearne (9)
Westrop Primary School, Swindon

Jurassic Chaos

In a mysterious park there were the most Jurassic beasts you would ever see. The dinosaurs. Today it was interestingly hot and something didn't feel right. Suddenly there were staff rushing to the laboratory. A dinosaur had broken out! It was the velociraptor. So some dinosaur hunters ran in. 'Argh!' screamed one of them, as he got snatched and was swallowed down the velociraptor's throat. After that there was silence...

William Hemns (9)
Westrop Primary School, Swindon

Wolf Dangers

With one fleshy thread hanging, Lily heard a blood curdling scream coming from the other side of the enchanted forest. So she sprinted quickly to where the sun beamed from the leather like treetops, and she found a threatened looking bunny lying on it's side in a puddle of its own blood. She carefully placed the three legged bunny into her checked scarf and carried it home. Her demented stepmother said she was not allowed to keep the bunny.
The next day her evil stepmother threw it back into the forest, and it was never seen again!

Tui Bettina Jasmine Jackson (8)
Westrop Primary School, Swindon

The Dark Shadows Of Black!

On an enchanted island of mysterious dreams a girl with wings was flying gracefully through the beautiful sky wondering what was behind the deadly black wall. With thunder of fright in her head there was a terrifying sound of a death scream. She flew away to the calm ground and thought whatever it was might get her next! She didn't know how she got there but she wanted to know more about the dark place.
Then surprisingly a ghost suddenly flew out and started chasing her and she screamed for help! Then she realised it had all been a dream.

Maisy McSharry (8)
Westrop Primary School, Swindon

Brooklyn Outbreak

In the middle of Brooklyn a zombie apocalypse had just broken out. Sean was an engineer at the time so he had a gun of course. He shot at the zombie but its arm held on by a thread. Sean ran and ran, then something occurred to him, he was dreaming. He was going to be fine! Or was he... 'Argh!' He's dead...

Jack Harris (9)
Westrop Primary School, Swindon

A Monster's Rage

In a ghostly forest a monster fifty storeys high with a tail of a scorpion and a body of a spider was capturing all the creatures in leathery webs, also poisoning all sorts. Two teenagers armed with pistols, swords and axes chose to hurt the beast. One died so the other pushed the monster off a cliff and was stabbed in the back with a rock. When he was going home he found that the land was healing so he was thinking, *will my friend come back?* Only time will tell, will he have to do more before he returns?

Hadley Chappell-Palmer (10)
Westrop Primary School, Swindon

Jurassic Park

Suddenly, someone called Joe entered a park called Jurassic Park.
Then Joe met some of his friends Jon-Joe, Jake and Harry. Joe
said, 'Do you want to go to the T-rex?'
Jon-Joe said, 'Yes let's go, come on let's go?'
The boys heard an enormous roar from the T-rex. It was because it
was fighting other dinosaurs.

Keelan Cornish (8)
Westrop Primary School, Swindon

The Russian Attack!

'The end is coming!' Sorry can't talk to you right now, Russians
attacking, got to move quickly, seriously! The camp he's got to
move. Oh and by the way my name is Chi-Chi, leader of the camp.
'Chi-Chi shelter over here!' pointed out one of the campers.
Later that day there were voices of people talking, the Russians!
Next, something not very nice happened, down went the door
and the Chinese prison campers died while trying to escape the
battlefield. The Russians had won the war. A very horrible one. The
Russians had won again. The Chinese campers were unlucky.

George Mack (9)
Westrop Primary School, Swindon

The Unfortunate Man

The girl was falling, her name was Ruby. Secretly she loved George and he loved her. Ruby's friends Sophie, Rosie and Poppy were worried. Suddenly George turned up but unfortunately fell into his doom. As quickly as a cheetah Ruby grabbed the rope out of George's pocket and threw it up to Sophie.

Sophie caught it, she pulled it up. Ruby was back up and safe. She was very scared because the mountain was a hundred foot tall. George looked down, wished he wasn't dead. Princess Ruby kept on thinking about Prince George. She was sad, she started to cry.

Chloe May Jones (9)
Westrop Primary School, Swindon

The Haunted House

My daughter and I were alone in my new house, we walked up the stairs into the bedroom and put our bags down. Suddenly one of my bags levitated into the air, I was shocked to find out that we were living with ghosts. Soon we began to know each other and we liked each other so much we decided to get married.

On the wedding day when we kissed I realised I was a ghost and so was my daughter. I was amazed by this, I couldn't believe it, I was a ghost!

Alfie Gunn (8)
Westrop Primary School, Swindon

The Haunted School Of Music

In Los Angeles it was a bright and sunny day, but one thing wasn't, the music school. Students who went there thought it was haunted. There were five teenagers and they also thought the school was haunted as well, but suddenly more blood dripped down the walls and a knife was hung up on the wall. The five teenagers were scared to death, but they just realised that Jade wasn't with them. No she was a ghost. 'Don't hurt us please, but why are you doing this Jade? Stop!' All four of them were dead. Jade was evil, pure evil.

Lily Grace Middleton (9)
Westrop Primary School, Swindon

Into The Woods

As she was quickly running Monty could smell the horrific stench of the giant's breath hammering down on her. Suddenly the giant flung Monty against the mountain, Monty struggled to survive the impact. She began breathing heavily. At that very moment he fell to the ground and the mud swallowed her whole! The giant searched the bean garden and the candy cottage! 'Cut, that's a wrap,' screeched the director. But the strange thing was when they went to pull Monty out she was nowhere to be seen and she was never seen again.

Rosie Percival (9)
Westrop Primary School, Swindon

The Wedding

In the distance two princesses were wishing they could go out of the castle gates. In the haunted house lives two vampires who wanted the kingdom for themselves. The kingdom was beautiful with happiness.

The next day one of the princesses fell in love with a prince and got married. The vampires used their magic and the vampires broke the crystal. People ran and the vampires and the princesses had a battle and the princesses won the battle.

Megan Close (7)
Westrop Primary School, Swindon

Mutantninja33's Quest

It all started a long time ago when there was a man called Mutantninja33 who discovered a portal. He went through it and went into a new dimension. It was all black. There was a temple under the sea and he went there and saw some fish. He slowly approached the fish but the fish turned round, its eyes turned red and started to attack him. He got out his sword and chopped him in half. He found some diamonds and emeralds. There was a dart trap and he died but he respawned.

Jamey Punchard (8)
Westrop Primary School, Swindon

The Haunted House

It was 1915, a family moved to a different house, they didn't know that it was a haunted house. A boy came into his room and it was a small room. When George went inside, the door slammed and he was trapped and the light was coming on and off. The boy was terrified so he ran to every corner and then he stood in the middle and then the lights went off. When they came on the boy disappeared, then nobody could find George and nobody ever saw him again.

Natalie Reinhold (8)
Westrop Primary School, Swindon

The Trenches

Bullets flying at Sir Tom, he poked his head up. Suddenly Jack the German shot him, it missed, luckily it was a rifle. Sir Tom got his machine-gun, he had a hundred shots until he reloaded. He shot and he was dead. *Bang!* He was dead. *Ding, ding,* the war was over. 'Thank God it is over!' said Sir Tom's mum, she knew that Sir Tom was dead because it had been a week so Sir Tom was dead or was he...

Louie Horan (8)
Westrop Primary School, Swindon

The Haunted Bathtub

Once there was a man, who was in the bath, called Alfie Gibbins, when he was finished he undid the plug and he sat in the bath, then he got sucked up by the bath and went down the plug and through the pipe and landed in the sewer. He swam to the edge of the sewer and found a rope, he picked it up and tied a loop in it. He saw the pipe and pulled himself up and he found some super boots. Then he jumped up the pipe and he came to his bath.

Harry Orchard (8)
Wool CE Primary School, Wareham

Candy Crush Saga

It was a hot summer's day, Little Miss Ginger was making her house out of her favourite treats, ginger sponge, icing and lollies. It was so hot that day, Little Miss Ginger's house melted down. Mrs Bubble Gum came and saw her house had melted. 'Shouldn't you be cleaning up?' Mrs Bubble Gum asked.
'Well yeah, where will I put it?'
'You'll see a bin? That's your plan?'
'Yeah, it's fine.'
'Okay.' So they put everything in the bin and Little Miss Ginger stayed at Mrs Bubble Gum's house made of gummy bears and swirly lollipops.

Ruby Sue Leaton (9)
Wool CE Primary School, Wareham

Super Monkey

Once upon a time before television there was a superhero, he had banana boomerangs, he could climb walls and even go upside down and he had super strength, his name was Super Monkey. One peaceful day the sun was out, but suddenly it started to rain, there was only one person behind this, Mr Evil. Super Monkey went to his tall big lair, it was dry there, Super Monkey investigated, he used his sticky power to sneak up on Mr Evil. He threw his banana boomerang and it hit the machine. He took Mr Evil away forever and ever.

Cohen Lee (9)
Wool CE Primary School, Wareham

Dino World

One sunny bright day there lived dinosaurs. They are nasty reptiles but these ones were kind. There lived this crazy caveman called Grug, he could speak but in a strange way. The herbivores were really good but for the T-rexs, they had to be fed by Grug. But there was one big problem, whenever the T-rexs are meat they went mad as a chicken on one leg, *cluck!* But Grub agreed that the T-rexs should eat grass instead of meat so they wouldn't get crazy again. Then the T-rexs tried it and they lived in Dino World forever.

Reuben Adams (9)
Wool CE Primary School, Wareham

Easter Egg Land

One Egg morning an egg called Dave was strolling along the yellow path but Dave noticed something was wrong, the path ended in front of him and there was a human in the land. Two hours later the human started to be quite a nice human and he had a banana called Bob. Bob was very odd. He played spinning plates and he was stupid. They went to a land of minions through a portal. They all went back to Egg Land and they built their village and they built a Statue of Liberty. They lived happily ever after.

Callum James Dicker (9)
Wool CE Primary School, Wareham

The Haunted Toilet

One day there lived a toilet plunger, he smelt like rotting fish. When he was having his lunch the phone suddenly rang. 'I need a toilet plunger.'
'Yes that's me, that will be hundred-ten pounds.'
'That will be fine.' He hung up. He hurried to investigate and the witch came to the door, he was frightened. He went to the bathroom and started to unblock the toilet but it sucked him down! It was disgusting down there and there were lots of other plunger men.
'Are you plunger men?'
'Yes we are,' they said and they lived happily ever after!

Theo Northover
Wool CE Primary School, Wareham

Chopped Wood

Once there was a boy called Luke, he did karate, he was very good at school. He was very nervous when it turned to July because his grading was next week and he was getting his black belt. He had to chop three planks of wood in half with his hand. The problem with this was he could only chop one plank of wood so he had to practise all day, all night. Finally it came to Saturday, he was next to chop the wood. He was up, he chopped the wood so hard it went through the roof! *Bang!*

Kieran Elford (9)
Wool CE Primary School, Wareham

The Wolves And The Dragon

One day three wolf friends were playing in a meadow, their names were Wolfie, Heater and Snowy. 'Isn't this fun girls?' asked Wolfie. 'Yep!' said the girls. Suddenly, a massive pack of gangster wolves showed up!
'Hey Wolfie, we're gonna rule this hill and kick you out!' said the leader.
'I don't think so!' shouted a dragon from above. Suddenly, there was a massive burst of purple smoke and the pack ran away.
'Weeellll that happened!' said Wolfie, then they all laughed together and became friends.

Keeley Harvey (9)
Wool CE Primary School, Wareham

Double Trouble

One day Harry and Steve were world champions also known as the Turbo Twins.
Today they were going to race on Mars against their cousins but when the race started they saw another spaceship, it looked like a cartoon one, it was yellow. When the Turbo Twins came home they found out it was aliens, they called the army, they said they were no threat.
Two months later the aliens invaded Earth, the lasers went *bang!*
Kaboom! The Turbo Twins said to the aliens, 'If we win the race, you will leave us alone.'

Alfie Gibbins-Goringe (8)
Wool CE Primary School, Wareham

Untitled

One day a girl called Shana was climbing Mount Everest for a race. As soon as she was in first place the people down below started to fall. She was still going. Suddenly the rocks started to fall on her so she let go but she was hanging on by the rope. 'Help!' she shouted. Suddenly *bang!* She fell. Later an ambulance arrived and took Shana away.
The next day she had a lot of get well soon cards, flowers and presents.
One month later Shana was better and was allowed to go home.

Hollie Scott (9)
Wool CE Primary School, Wareham

The Unforgettable World

Once upon a time in New York City there was a disaster; dragons, dinosaurs, giants, witches, wizards and dwarfs destroyed the world. It was time for Spider-Man to fix the world. 'Wow!' said Spider-Man. 'I need to make a plan.'
The next day Spider-Man saw a little girl stuck in dinosaur poop and was about to get eaten. Spider-Man saved the little girl and killed the dragons, dinosaurs, giants, witches, wizards and dwarfs! So the world was back to normal. But Spider-Man was upset because no one congratulated him then *boom!* They started a party in his honour.

Sasha Daly (8)
Wool CE Primary School, Wareham

The Man In The Zoo

Once there was a man called Jeff, he was going on a boat and he slipped off the edge and fell off the boat. When he got to the middle of the water it was misty and then he turned around to see the boat so he got back on it and then saw land. He saw some knights guarding the zoo from the lion. It roared and most of the knights got away. Jeff stopped the knights and put the lion in a cage and the zookeeper gave him a card to say thanks.

James Michael Harkin (8)
Wool CE Primary School, Wareham

Football Friday

Once upon a time a boy called Jeff was in his garden playing football when he heard the postman, it was Friday. 'Yay!' Jeff shouted. He was getting a new football kit, he was excited.
The next day he woke up at five o'clock in the morning so he could play football. Then he realised the kit had gone. He got changed really quickly and went downstairs so he could rush out the door to find it. But he looked everywhere. When he went back home he found it in the washing machine being washed.

Alex Hollingum (8)
Wool CE Primary School, Wareham

YOUNG WRITERS INFORMATION

We hope you have enjoyed reading this book – and that you will continue to in the coming years.

If you're a young writer who enjoys reading and creative writing, or the parent of an enthusiastic poet or story writer, do visit our website www.youngwriters.co.uk. Here you will find free competitions, workshops and games, as well as recommended reads, a poetry glossary and our blog.

If you would like to order further copies of this book, or any of our other titles, give us a call or visit **www.youngwriters.co.uk.**

Young Writers, Remus House
Coltsfoot Drive, Peterborough, PE2 9BF

(01733) 890066 / 898110
info@youngwriters.co.uk